*She froze as the car
aimed right for her.*

Just as she started to cross her driveway, the lights hit her.

Bright lights. Aimed right at her. Melanie squinted. All she saw was fog, swirling around two yellow lights.

Then Melanie heard a low, rumbling noise.

Suddenly, the engine roared. The car shot forward, its lights piercing the fog.

Melanie stood frozen in the glare like a deer on a highway.

Other Thrillers
you will enjoy:

*Silent Witness*
by Carol Ellis

*Twins*
by Caroline B. Cooney

*The Train*
by Diane Hoh

*The Phantom*
by Barbara Steiner

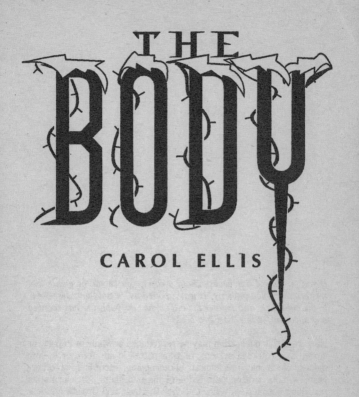

# THE BODY

## CAROL ELLIS

SCHOLASTIC INC.
New York Toronto London Auckland Sydney

No part of this publication may be reproduced in whole or in part, or stored in a retrieval system, or transmitted in any form or by any means, electronic, mechanical, photocopying, recording, or otherwise, without written permission of the publisher. For information regarding permission, write to Scholastic Inc., 555 Broadway, New York, NY 10012.

ISBN 0-590-48156-8

12 11 10 9 8 7 6 5 4 3 2 1          5 6 7 8 9/9 0/0

Printed in the U.S.A.                              01

First Scholastic printing, April 1995

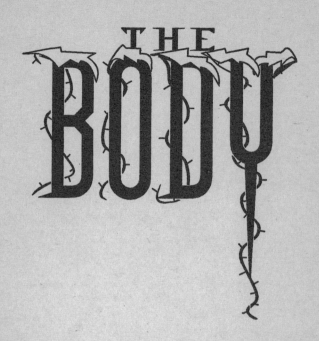

# Prologue

She hadn't forgotten. Even with her body so filled with pain that her mind had closed itself to everything else, the memory was there, just waiting to surface. When it did, she wanted to scream.

The memory came back whole, not in bits and pieces. She saw the faces, heard the shouts, felt the breath rasping in her throat as she ran.

She hadn't screamed then. She *couldn't* scream now. Now it was too late.

But what she had seen was still trapped inside her. It had to be told. She had to think of a way, but she had to be careful.

And when she did tell, she wondered if she'd finally scream.

# Chapter 1

The newspaper ad was short and to the point. *Wanted*, it said. *Reader. Reliable, responsible. Flexible hours.*

That's me, Melanie Jacobs thought when she saw it. She hadn't discovered any great hidden talents about herself yet. But she could read. She was reliable. And she could use some extra money.

When Melanie answered the ad, the woman on the phone had a cool, clipped voice, but Melanie thought she heard a hint of relief in it. Maybe nobody else had called about the job, which turned out to be reading to an invalid for about an hour a day. The pay was decent.

*Drive up the cliff road*, the woman had said. *When you can't go any farther, you're there. It's the Randolph house.*

It was gray and foggy when Melanie left her own house and drove through the streets of

Clifton, Massachusetts. Almost every morning since she'd moved here a few weeks before had been gray and foggy. This Monday was no exception.

Melanie had been furious when her parents decided to move. All her friends were back in Kansas. She'd asked — begged — to stay behind and live with one of these friends, just until she finished high school. No deal.

So she was a stranger in a strange town. She'd be a stranger when school started in September. She would be friendless. She wouldn't belong.

When Melanie finally saw the house, she stopped and stared. Its pale-gray stone walls seemed built from the wisps of fog that still clung to the ground around it. It was three stories tall, and stood close to the edge of the cliffs overlooking the town.

Even though it was June, Melanie shivered. The house was like something out of a horror movie. A bad horror movie. Invalid or not, she'd feel like a prisoner living there.

Melanie tightened her grip on the wheel of the car and looked around. Ahead, between two flat-topped pillars, she could see the front of the house. A short, U-shaped drive ran up to the wide front door. It was black and shiny, with a big stone urn on each side. The urns were empty. They needed flowers or ivy in them. Something alive.

The woman had told Melanie to drive to the back. What she really wanted to do was turn around and leave. It was too eerie here.

Shake it off, she told herself. You need the job. You need something to do besides sit around in an empty house, feeling sorry for yourself because you had to move. She drove forward.

She didn't see the other car until it was almost too late.

Bright red, it shot out between the gray pillars like a torch, missing Melanie's front bumper by inches.

Hitting the horn and the brakes at the same time, Melanie swerved to a stop.

The red car didn't even slow down. Melanie caught a glimpse of the driver behind the wheel — his lips parted as if he were yelling at her; his face partially covered by black aviator sunglasses. A spray of gravel rattled against her fender, and then the car was gone, fishtailing around a curve in the cliff road.

Shaken and furious, Melanie leaned her head back and took a deep breath.

It wasn't a good omen.

Maybe she should just forget it and go home, *now*.

No, she thought stubbornly. No!

Still angry, she drove between the pillars and down the curved, tree-lined drive around to the back of the house. In a wide parking area next to a triple garage, she pulled to a stop alongside a dark-green pickup truck loaded with yard tools.

Melanie got out and looked around. The back of the house had tall windows that looked out on a stone terrace with a waist-high wall. On top of the wall was a black and white cat, lying on its back. When Melanie slammed her car door, the cat turned onto its stomach to watch her.

Steps from the terrace led down to a sloping green lawn. Beyond, a thick tangle of trees seemed to go on forever. Wisps of fog drifted like smoke through the trees. It was very quiet.

Too quiet.

Out of the corner of her eye, Melanie saw a shadow move across the windows. She turned, then jumped as a high-pitched whine suddenly cut through the silence. The cat came to life, springing from the wall and streaking around a corner of the house. Forgetting about the shadow at the window, Melanie spun around and saw a bare-chested man in jeans trimming a hedge on the far side of the lawn.

Stop letting this place get to you, Melanie told herself.

Feeling foolish for spooking so easily, Melanie smoothed back her shoulder-length, light-brown hair. She started up the wide flagstone walk leading to a door at one end of the terrace. Before she reached it, the door opened. A tall, fortyish woman with dark hair and perfect posture stood there. She watched silently as Melanie picked her way up the puddled walk.

"Mrs. Randolph?" Melanie said when she got closer.

The woman's mouth curved slightly. Melanie decided it was a smile, even though it looked more like a sneer. "I'm Ms. Hudson," the woman said. "Georgia Hudson."

Melanie recognized her voice from the telephone call. "Sorry," she said. "I didn't get your name when we talked. I'm Melanie Jacobs. You probably already guessed that."

Georgia Hudson nodded and stepped aside so Melanie could go into the house.

"This way, please," Ms. Hudson said.

Melanie followed the woman down a long, dim hallway. They passed several carved wooden doors, and a hall that led to another wing of the house. Melanie had never been in a place this big before. Was Georgia Hudson the housekeeper? Whoever she was, she wasn't much for small talk.

Stopping at one of the carved doors, Ms. Hudson opened it and led Melanie into a small room with ivy-patterned wallpaper. In it were two chairs, a desk, a computer, and several file cabinets. A small television sat on the desk.

Ms. Hudson moved behind the desk and motioned for Melanie to take one of the chairs. She said, as if she'd been reading Melanie's thoughts, "I manage the house for the Randolphs. I have an apartment upstairs here. Stuart — Mr. Randolph — is a consultant for several large businesses and he's away a lot. I'm also his personal secretary."

A housekeeper/secretary, Melanie thought. She'd been close.

"Do you know Mr. Randolph?" Ms. Hudson asked.

"No," Melanie said. "I haven't lived in Clifton very long."

"Oh, yes, that's right. I had to give you directions," the housekeeper said. "So you don't know Lisa Randolph, either."

Melanie shook her head. "Is she . . . ?"

"She had an accident. She's paralyzed."

"Oh. I'm sorry." It sounded pretty lame, but Melanie couldn't think of anything else to say.

"Yes. Everyone is." Georgia Hudson picked up a pencil and started to fiddle with it. Then she put it down. "The doctors think it's possible for her to recover," she said. "A physical therapist visits her regularly, so do some of her friends." Her mouth twitched in that sneer/smile again. Melanie got the feeling that Georgia Hudson wasn't crazy about Lisa Randolph's friends.

"But she needs more," the housekeeper went on. "She always enjoyed reading, but she can't do it on her own now. The doctor suggested hiring a reader." She looked at Melanie with her hooded dark eyes and changed the subject. "Tell me about yourself, Melanie."

"Well, I moved here a few weeks ago," Melanie said. "I'm seventeen. I'll be a senior when school starts. I've been baby-sitting at a neighbor's, but I'd like to earn a little more money. Most of the summer jobs are already taken, so when I saw the ad, I called." Listening to herself, Melanie didn't think she sounded very impressive. But the woman didn't want to hear her life story. She just wanted somebody who could read.

Ms. Hudson stared out the window. Following her gaze, Melanie saw the bare-chested gardener walking along the side yard. He was younger than he'd looked at a distance. Maybe her own age, she thought. Dark hair poked out from under his baseball cap.

As if he knew he was being watched, the guy turned and looked into the window. Melanie wasn't sure, but she thought he smiled.

Looking annoyed, Georgia Hudson got up and pulled a heavy green curtain across the window. Then she sat back down and folded her hands on top of the desk. "Reading aloud to someone isn't as easy as it sounds," she said. "I tried it with Lisa, and even though I tried to keep my voice animated, I'm afraid I failed. And, frankly, I don't have the time. Maybe you can do better. Why don't you come meet her now? Talk to her a little, read a little. If it goes well, then we'll discuss what times would be best for both of you."

A tryout, Melanie thought. Why not? The worst that could happen was that she'd put herself and Lisa Randolph to sleep. Of course, she wouldn't get the job, then, but maybe that wouldn't be so bad after all.

The place gave her an uneasy feeling.

Ms. Hudson was already at the door. As Melanie stood up, a man came in. Dressed in a dark business suit, he looked about the same age as the housekeeper. He also looked as if he had a lot on his mind.

"Georgia, I need — " the man stopped talking when he saw Melanie.

"Mr. Randolph, this is Melanie Jacobs," Ms. Hudson said. "She answered the newspaper ad."

"Oh? Good." Stuart Randolph stuck out his hand and Melanie shook it. She thought he'd say something about the job, but instead, he quickly turned back to the housekeeper. "I need to talk to you as soon as you finish here," he said. "It's important."

"Of course." Ms. Hudson smiled. This time the smile was genuine, Melanie noticed.

"Okay. Fine." With another quick glance at Melanie, Stuart Randolph left, his footsteps echoing down the polished wood floor of the hallway.

Georgia Hudson fluffed up her dark hair and looked at her watch. Her cheeks were tinged with pink. "This way, please."

Melanie followed her down the long hallway again, toward the back of the house. When they reached the large wooden doors, Ms. Hudson stopped. "I should tell you," she said. "Lisa doesn't speak. The doctors aren't sure of the cause." She opened the door and stood aside for Melanie to go in.

The room was big. And even on a gray day it should have been filled with light. Four windows at the back reached almost from floor to ceiling and looked out on the stone terrace. There were three more tall windows on the far side.

But in spite of the windows, it was dark. Maybe it was the heavy bookcases lining two of the walls. Or the dark wood-and-leather furniture, or the stone-cold fireplace.

It should have been a beautiful room, full of warmth. But all Melanie could think of was the feeling she'd had when she first saw the house — like she was looking at a prison.

Now, she was looking at the prisoner: a girl her own age, sitting in a wheelchair in the middle of a cold, dark room.

# Chapter 2

Melanie knew she was staring, but she couldn't look away.

One hand in her lap, the other on the arm of the chair, the girl looked back out of light-brown eyes that had little flecks of gold in them. She was dressed in a long yellow robe like a beach cover-up. Her dark-brown hair was pulled away from her face by two tortoiseshell combs. There was a fading bruise on one cheek, and a dark scab running through her eyebrow up to her hairline. The part of her neck that Melanie could see had a thin red line on it that looked painful. But even trapped in a wheelchair and unable to move, she was the brightest thing in the room.

"Lisa, this is Melanie Jacobs," Ms. Hudson said, striding into the room and over to the wheelchair. "She's come to read to you. That'll be nice, won't it?"

The housekeeper's voice had changed. She was talking in a false, bright, singsong tone that grated on Melanie's nerves, as if Lisa were a three-year-old.

Standing behind the wheelchair now, Ms. Hudson gestured to Melanie. "Come say hello."

Melanie moved farther into the room and stopped a couple of feet from the wheelchair. "Hi, Lisa," she said with a smile. "Ms. Hudson told me you like to read. I've never read like this before, so I hope I'm okay at it. Anyway, what do you like . . . ?" Melanie stopped, blushing. Hadn't the housekeeper said Lisa couldn't talk? Or didn't talk? Melanie felt incredibly stupid for starting off with a question.

Melanie glanced at Georgia Hudson. "Don't worry about it, just keep talking," the housekeeper said, checking her watch. "Get acquainted."

Taking a breath, Melanie smiled at Lisa again. "Well, I'm seventeen," she said. "And I'm new in town. My dad's the new principal at the middle school and my mom's a veterinarian. She wants to open an office here, but she hasn't found a place yet." Melanie rattled on, unable to stop. "My brother David's twenty — he's hiking in Europe this summer with his girlfriend."

Melanie stopped, out of breath. Had Lisa's eyes changed? Widened? Or darkened? Was she bored already?

Georgia Hudson cleared her throat. "Why don't you find a book?" she suggested. Her voice was losing its brightness — *she* was definitely bored. And impatient to get to the meeting with her boss.

"Right. Good idea." Melanie walked over to a wall of books and started scanning the titles. Lots of law stuff. Two sets of encyclopedias and dozens of other reference books.

Stooping down, Melanie spotted a whole row of science fiction paperbacks. She looked over her shoulder at Lisa. "You like sci-fi?" she asked, hoping Lisa didn't. Melanie had never been able to get into it.

"I don't think so," Ms. Hudson answered. "That's what I read to her. Her mother liked them, that's why I picked one."

Nobody had mentioned a *Mrs.* Randolph. Melanie decided not to ask.

Moving on, Melanie passed a bunch of spy novels, and a few books of poetry. Then she saw a row of leather-bound classics. Their titles were stamped in gold on the books' spines. One of the books was Charlotte Brontë's *Jane Eyre*.

"Hey!" she said, pulling it out. "I read this

last year. Well, I *had* to read it. For school. But I really liked it."

Lisa's brownish-gold eyes moved over the gold-stamped words on the book Melanie held up.

"Quite a coincidence," Georgia Hudson said. "Lisa was reading that book shortly before her accident. I believe it may have been one of the choices on the reading list for senior year."

"Really?" Melanie looked at Lisa. "Did you like it?"

Lisa raised her gaze to Melanie's face.

"I don't remember her saying anything about it." Ms. Hudson looked at her watch again. Just as she did, the door opened and Stuart Randolph walked in.

Lisa's glance shifted to her father's face. Melanie thought her eyes changed again, as if a shadow had moved across them . . . a plea of some kind.

"Hey, honey." Mr. Randolph walked over to the wheelchair and dropped a kiss on his daughter's head. Then he turned. "Georgia, are you just about finished? I've got a plane to catch and we need to go over some things."

"Ms. Hudson, why don't I go ahead and start reading while you're with Mr. Randolph?"

Melanie said quickly. It would be easier to do it alone, anyway.

"Yes, that's a good idea," Ms. Hudson said, sounding relieved. "You get started and I'll be back in a few minutes."

Mr. Randolph kissed Lisa's head again. "See you in a couple of days, honey," he said. Then he strode to the door with Georgia Hudson right behind him.

When the door shut, Melanie held the book in front of Lisa again. "You sure this is okay?" she asked. Melanie didn't expect an answer, but she thought she should ask, anyway.

Melanie grabbed an overstuffed ottoman in front of one of the leather chairs and dragged it across the floor to the wheelchair. The chair was angled so that Lisa could look out the tall windows at the end of the room. The black and white cat was back on the wall, Melanie noticed. She pulled the ottoman around in front of the chair and sat, her back to the windows.

A dark-red ribbon was sewn into the binding as a bookmark. Melanie assumed this was where Lisa had been before the accident. She opened the book to the ribbon and scanned the page. "Oh, this is where Jane saves Mr. Rochester from being burned in his bed." She flipped back a couple of pages. "Right, first she hears somebody outside her door in the middle of the night." Melanie looked up. "I'll start here."

Lisa kept staring straight ahead.

Melanie cleared her throat and took a breath. *"I tried again to sleep; but my heart beat anxiously: my inward tranquillity was broken. The clock, far down in the hall, struck two. Just then, it seemed my chamber door was touched; as if fingers had swept the panels in a groping way along the dark gallery outside. I said, 'who is there?' Nothing answered. I was chilled with fear."*

Melanie paused and looked up from the book. Lisa's eyes had narrowed, as if she were listening closely. Melanie hoped it was that, and not that Lisa was getting sleepy already. She went on reading.

*"All at once, I remembered that it might be Pilot: who, when the kitchen-door chanced to be left open, not unfrequently found his way up to the threshold of Mr. Rochester's chamber."*

Melanie paused again. "Pilot's the dog," she said. "Just in case you forgot." She started to read again, then shifted around on the ottoman. "Sorry," she said. "I can't seem to get comfortable." As she settled down, she realized what that must have sounded like. *She* couldn't get comfortable? But she felt she understood what Lisa must be feeling. Trapped. She felt trapped, herself, in Clifton.

Flustered and embarrassed, Melanie picked up the book. Just read, she told herself.

After a few more lines, Melanie stopped worrying about how she sounded, or whether she was reading too fast or not fast enough. It was an exciting part of the book, and she got caught up in it the way she had when she'd first read it. She shivered at the "marrow-freezing," demonlike laugh outside Jane's door. When Jane finds a candle burning in the hallway, Melanie read, *"I was surprised at this circumstance: but still more was I amazed to perceive the air quite dim, as if filled with smoke; and while looking to the right hand and left, I became further aware of a strong smell of burning."*

Melanie thought she heard Lisa breathe in sharply. But when she looked up quickly, Lisa was still. She went on reading about Jane Eyre seeing the smoke coming from Mr. Rochester's room; running in to find his bed burning; dousing it with water from his pitcher and bowl. A drenched Rochester finally wakes up, yelling about a flood.

" *'In the name of all the elves in Christendom, is that Jane Eyre?' he demanded. 'What have you done with me, witch, sorceress? Who* is in the room besides you? Have you plotted to drown me?' "

" 'I will fetch you a candle, sir; and, in Heaven's name, get up. Somebody has plotted something: you cannot too soon find out who and what it is.' "

Melanie stopped. A movement had caught her eye. Somewhere during the last two or three lines, Lisa had lifted the hand that was resting on the wheelchair; lifted it and brought it down on the padded arm.

Lisa's eyes were still narrowed. Behind the thick lashes, Melanie could see they were glittering.

Melanie almost said, "I thought you were paralyzed." But she caught herself in time. She hardly knew anything about paralysis, and Georgia Hudson hadn't told her any details. But Lisa couldn't be *totally* paralyzed. Obviously, Lisa could move a little.

Melanie couldn't imagine being like this, with some stranger talking at her. And *staring* at her, she realized with a blush.

Ducking her head, Melanie found her place again. "Right. *'I will fetch you a candle, sir; and, in Heaven's name, get up. Somebody has plotted something: you cannot too soon find out who and what it is.'* "

Taking a breath, Melanie started to go on.

But Lisa stopped her again, with the same movement of her hand — lifting it slightly from the wrist, then dropping it to the arm of the wheelchair.

"I . . . I'm sorry," Melanie said. "Are you getting tired?"

Lisa remained still.

"I'm not sure what to do," Melanie said, miserably. She thought she ought to do *something*. She marked her place with the red ribbon and closed the book. She gazed at Lisa, and ached for some help.

"Water," a voice said.

# Chapter 3

"Water."

Melanie spun around, looking at the back of Lisa's wheelchair. "Did you — "

"Try the water," the voice said. And this time Melanie recognized it. It belonged to Georgia Hudson, who was nowhere in the room.

As if she could see Melanie's confusion and thought it was amusing, the housekeeper chuckled dryly. "I'm talking over an intercom," she said. "I heard you, and I can see you, too."

"See me?"

"Closed-circuit TV. Didn't I tell you? There are cameras in several rooms and monitors in every room of the house, so we can keep an eye on Lisa," Ms. Hudson explained. "Not that she's ever alone for long. We have two cameras in the library because it's so big. One at each end of the room. See them?"

Melanie saw them now — one was on the far wall; one up above the tall windows at the back. She immediately tried to remember if she'd done anything embarrassing. Nice of Hudson to warn her, she thought sarcastically. Instead of watching the soaps with that TV on her desk, the housekeeper had been watching *her*.

She stared at the camera on the far wall, tempted to make a face at it. "You said something about water?"

"Yes. There's a carafe and glasses on a table on the far side of the room. Try giving her some water. What upset you, by the way?"

Two cameras and she had to ask? "Didn't you see?"

"This isn't a security setup — I only glance at the monitor periodically." Ms. Hudson sounded impatient. "What happened?"

"She moved her hand," Melanie said, hating to talk about Lisa as if she weren't there.

"Oh?" There was a pause. "Yes, I think I've seen that before. She does have *some* movement, mostly in her legs, though she can't walk yet." Ms. Hudson changed the subject quickly.

"Give her some water, then keep reading for awhile."

When the disembodied voice didn't say anything more, Melanie figured the housekeeper was finished. She poured some water for herself, gulped it down, and poured more into a second glass. There were several straws on the tray — the kind that bent and made Melanie think of disgusting caterpillars. She bent one, stuck it into the glass, and crossed the room to Lisa.

Knowing she was being watched made Melanie nervous and awkward. She wondered what Lisa thought about being on camera all the time. It must be awful for her . . . almost inhuman.

In front of the wheelchair again, Melanie smiled and raised her eyebrows. "I hope this is what you wanted," she said. She held the straw to Lisa's lips, then looked away while she drank. She didn't know how Lisa felt, but *she* wouldn't want anyone watching *her* drink.

When Lisa was finished, Melanie set the glass on a nearby table. As she picked up *Jane Eyre*, she saw that the gardener was up on the terrace, sweeping away damp leaves with a big broom. The black and white cat was hunkered down and watching, its tail flicking back and forth.

Suddenly the cat pounced at the leaves and then wrestled with the broom. The gardener leaned on the broom handle and watched the cat for a second, smiling. Then he glanced toward the tall windows. When he saw the two girls inside, his smile widened.

Sweeping the baseball cap off his dark hair, he bowed low, like an actor in an old-fashioned play. Then he jammed the cap back on, shouldered the broom, and turned away.

Melanie smiled and looked at Lisa, half-expecting her to be smiling, too. But Lisa's face was still. Only her eyes moved, following the gardener as he ran lightly down the stone steps and out of sight.

"He's cute, isn't he?" Melanie asked.

Lisa's eyes snapped back to her, and for some reason, Melanie suddenly remembered the cameras and the intercom. She glanced at the camera on the other side of the room and shrugged her shoulders. So what? He *was* cute.

"Okay, back to the nineteenth century." She picked up the book and found her place. She was eager to finish reading and get away from Lisa, and Ms. Hudson, and the creepy house.

"Okay, Jane just told Mr. Rochester that somebody's out to get him. That's pretty obvious, but he . . . well, never mind, I'll just read."

Melanie read for another fifteen minutes — through Jane's waiting all the next day, hoping to see Mr. Rochester again, and then suddenly learning that he was gone.

"Jane's got it bad, doesn't she?" Melanie said to Lisa. She was trying hard to talk to Lisa as normally as possible. "Jane's really falling for Rochester and now she learns he's gone to stay at an estate and the owner has two daughters, one beautiful, one gorgeous." Melanie scanned what was coming next and laughed. "Then she makes herself even more miserable by asking exactly what the gorgeous one looks like. Listen to this."

*"You saw her, you say, Mrs. Fairfax: What was she like?"*

Melanie read the Rochester housekeeper's description of a Christmas ball, and then went on, " . . . *but Miss Ingram was certainly the queen.*"

*"And what was she like?"*

*"Tall, fine bust, sloping shoulders; long, graceful neck; olive complexion, dark and clear; noble features; eyes rather like Mr. Rochester's*

*— large and black, and as brilliant as
her . . ."*

Melanie stopped reading suddenly.

Lisa was lifting her hand *again*. Exactly the
same way as before — up from the wrist, then
down on the arm of the wheelchair. Before
Melanie could ask if she wanted more water,
Lisa repeated the motion.

Not wanting Georgia Hudson's voice to
come blaring over the intercom, Melanie
quickly got up to get fresh water.

The table with the carafe was in front of the
side windows. Melanie hadn't noticed before,
but now she saw that these windows opened
like doors onto a set of long steps. The steps
led down to a side yard that sloped to a sharp
drop-off. This wide gash in the earth ran the
whole length of the house, all the way into the
woods. She stood on tiptoe and craned her
neck, but she couldn't see the bottom.

Back at the wheelchair, Melanie offered the
water. Lisa didn't make any move to drink.

Maybe she was tired, Melanie thought.
After all, she'd been reading for close to half
an hour.

Lisa's eyes shifted to the book, then back
to Melanie's face.

Melanie set the glass down, picked up the
book, and read three more pages, to the end

of the chapter. When she finished, her mouth was bone dry. She got another drink for herself and was gulping it down when the door opened and Ms. Hudson came in.

The housekeeper was followed by a woman in white nylon pants and tunic that made Melanie think of a visit to the dentist.

"Lisa," Georgia Hudson said brightly, "Mrs. Miles is here."

Mrs. Miles smiled, her teeth as white as her tunic. "Ready to work on those legs, Lisa?" she asked, walking around to stand in front of the wheelchair.

When Lisa saw Mrs. Miles, she closed her eyes. The physical therapist, Melanie thought.

"I know, reading's much nicer," Mrs. Miles said, patting Lisa's knee. She stood up and went behind the chair. "Come on, let's get to work. The sooner we do, the sooner it'll be over."

As Mrs. Miles pushed the chair toward Melanie, Melanie smiled. Lisa didn't. But her eyes were open now, wide and, until the chair was past Melanie, she kept staring into Melanie's. What does she *want*? Melanie thought.

A couple of minutes later, Melanie was back in Georgia Hudson's office, working out the reading schedule. She'd been hired.

She wasn't sure she really wanted the job. The place still gave her the shivers, and Lisa made her uncomfortable.

"Mrs. Miles comes two mornings a week," Ms. Hudson said as she checked her desk calendar. "The other three days, Lisa goes to the hospital for water therapy and such. That's always early in the morning. She's back here by ten."

"The afternoons must be kind of a drag for her, then," Melanie said.

"Yes. You're probably right."

What did Lisa do on those long afternoons? Melanie wondered. Sit in front of a television. Listen to the radio? Cry? "Where is Lisa's mother?" Melanie asked tentatively. "I guess it's none of my business, but I can't help wondering."

Ms. Hudson looked like she agreed that it wasn't Melanie's business. But she said, "She divorced Mr. Randolph six years ago and died in a car crash four years ago. Now, about your reading time."

No mother, a father who was away a lot, a housekeeper who was about as warm and friendly as a Doberman. Melanie decided to take the job for awhile, anyway. She could always quit. But Lisa was imprisoned here. It made Melanie ache for her. "Why don't I come around two?" she said.

"Fine." The housekeeper scribbled on her calendar and stood up. She smiled, but it was a cool smile, like her voice. She walked Melanie to the back of the house and showed her out. "Tomorrow, then. And thank you."

Melanie said good-bye and stared down the walk. It was dry now, and the sun was trying to break through the clouds. She felt her mood lift as she headed for the car, as if she were escaping from something painful.

Poor Lisa.

At the end of the walk, Melanie turned and looked back at the library windows. She half-expected to see Lisa Randolph there, sitting in the wheelchair and staring out at the dark forest beyond the lawn. She had the feeling that Lisa spent a lot of time in that room, staring. Doing nothing.

"I know what you're thinking," a voice behind her said. "You're thinking those vines need pulling down."

Melanie turned around. It was the gardener. He was now wearing a faded-blue T-shirt. He had dark-brown eyes to go with his dark-brown hair.

Melanie smiled. "What vines?"

He pointed toward the library. "The ones

growing up the wall there, between the windows."

"I didn't even notice them," Melanie said.

"Yeah, that's the problem with them. One day there's just a shoot or two. Then you turn your back and they've got the house wrapped up. Vines are no good. For houses," he added with a grin. "So what were you thinking about?"

"Oh. About Lisa," Melanie said. "I just got hired to read to her."

"Hired?" He looked at the library again, then back at Melanie. "You're not a friend of hers?" he asked.

"No, I just moved to Clifton," Melanie said.

"I'm new here, too. Jeff Singer," he said, holding out his hand and smiling into her eyes.

"Melanie Jacobs." She liked the way his hand felt. Rough with callouses, but warm. His smile was great. "If you're new, then I guess you don't know much about Lisa, either," she said. "Do you know what happened? Ms. Hudson just told me she had an accident."

Jeff's face changed. "She fell off the cliff," he answered brusquely. "I don't know how."

It was clear he didn't intend to say anything more.

"Oh." Melanie didn't know what else to say.

Whatever Jeff *did* know about the accident, he wasn't going to tell *her*.

"So what do you think of Georgia the Gatekeeper?" Jeff asked, changing the subject.

"Not much," Melanie said bluntly. "She's cold. Like the house. Actually, when you came up, I was thinking maybe I could read to Lisa on the terrace sometimes. If you promise not to let the vines strangle us," she added.

"That's my job." Jeff frowned, and for a second, Melanie thought she'd insulted him somehow. But then he said, "I hope you can talk Hudson into it. I opened one of those French windows the other day — it wasn't locked — to sweep away some of the pine needles and debris. Lisa was in the room alone. About five seconds later, Hudson was out on the terrace giving me the third degree. Why had I opened the window? Did I want 'Miss Randolph' to catch a chill?" He shook his head. "Actually, I thought the fresh air might be good for her, but I didn't say so. I'm pretty sure Hudson thought I was planning to rob the place. I still haven't figured out how she knew what I'd done."

"Cameras. They're all over," Melanie said. She told him what had happened when Lisa moved her hand, and described the camera setup. "I guess it's a good idea," she added.

"But I wish Ms. Hudson had warned me."

He nodded, still looking at the house. His mind was somewhere else again.

"Well." Melanie cleared her throat. "I'm going to go."

"What? Oh." His eyes snapped back to her. "Okay. I'll probably see you again." He reached out and pulled a pine needle from Melanie's hair. He was smiling once more. "I'm here a lot," he said. Then he turned and headed across the lawn.

Melanie watched him for a few seconds. Why did he change like that? Tense and almost angry one second. Smiling and flirting the next. A little scary. But sexy. She liked the way he moved. Loose-limbed, but not gangly.

Georgia the Gatekeeper probably couldn't stand him.

Back in her car, Melanie rolled down the window and pulled around Jeff's truck. Her stomach growled and she realized she was starving. Maybe she'd stop and get a cheeseburger. And a milkshake. Or pizza.

Thinking about food, she drove a little faster down the long curving drive toward the stone pillars at the entrance. Then she saw a car turn in.

It was the same red car Melanie had seen earlier.

It was coming right at her.

Melanie slammed her hand against the horn. If this was a game of chicken, she didn't want to play.

But the red car kept coming.

And there was nowhere for her to turn.

# Chapter 4

Melanie jammed on the brake. Her car fish-tailed. Tightening both hands on the wheel, she fought to control it.

With a shriek of its tires, the red car swerved past and lurched to a halt. Melanie's car spun completely around and stopped.

Melanie was out of her car first. "That's the second time!" she yelled, slamming the door hard enough to rock the car. Furious, she stamped over and stood glaring at the driver as he scrambled out of his car.

He was tall, about her age, wearing fraying cutoffs and a loose orange T-shirt. His hair was dark blond and his eyes were hidden behind aviator glasses.

He was talking fast.

"Hey, I'm sorry! I don't know what happened! I mean, I look away for just a second to keep something from falling off the front seat and the next thing I know, my whole short life's flashing right in front of my eyes!" The words spilled out one on top of the other. With jerky, rapid gestures, he pushed the glasses on top of his head. His eyes were blue, with gray smudges underneath, as if he hadn't slept. "I'm sorry," he said again. "Really, it was my fault. You okay?"

"That's the *second* time you almost crashed into me!"

The young man peered over Melanie's shoulder at her car and snapped his fingers. "The gate! Right? About an hour ago, right?"

Melanie was still shaken and angry. But what good did it do to be angry at such an obvious lunatic?

"Forget it," she said, turning back to her car. "Just watch where you're going and try driving under eighty, okay?"

"Wait a sec, you gotta let me explain," he said. "I mean, I know it's not an excuse, but . . . wait, I'll be right back!" He dashed over to his car, reached inside and pulled out a bunch of yellow and white daisies wrapped in flimsy green paper. "These were about to fall off the front seat. And the floor's pretty grungy and I didn't want them to get messed up. So I looked over when I grabbed for them and . . . there you were!"

Melanie believed him, but it didn't make her feel all that forgiving. "What about before?" she asked. "When you almost plowed me off the cliff?"

"Oh. Well, I was mad." He held his hand up. "I know, I know — never take your anger out behind the wheel of a car." He smiled. "Driver's Ed — 101."

"You mean you *passed*?"

"Here." He pulled a white daisy out of the bunch and held it out to Melanie.

Melanie shook her head.

"Oh, come on. Take it," he said. "It's already out; I'll just break the stem if I try to get it back in."

"Okay." Melanie took the flower. "But I've already memorized your license plate, so watch out."

"Now you sound like Georgia Hudson."

Melanie grimaced. "Thanks a lot!"

He grinned. "You mean you don't like Sweet Georgia?"

"I guess I shouldn't complain about her. I hardly know her," Melanie said. "Besides, she just hired me."

"Hired you? What for?"

"To read to Lisa Randolph," Melanie said. "Do you know her?"

He looked toward the house. He lowered

his dark glasses over his eyes and, for a moment, was still. "Yeah, I know Lisa," he said at last. "We've been going together for almost a year."

"Oh. I'm sorry. I mean . . ." Melanie broke off and looked down at the daisy. "Are the flowers for her?"

"Yeah, Georgia wouldn't let me hang around before, that's why I was mad. The physical therapy's kind of hard on Lisa. So I took off to get her something to cheer her up." He took his eyes off the house and looked at Melanie. "I'm Garrett, by the way. Garrett Bailey."

"Melanie Jacobs."

"So. You're going to read to Lisa? That's good," Garrett said. "I tried it a couple of times, but I wasn't great at it. And then Lisa started blinking her eyes, and Hawkeye Hudson decided she was getting upset."

"Lisa moved her hand a few times when I was reading and Ms. Hudson saw it on her monitor," Melanie said. "She told me to give her some water."

"She moved her hand?" Garrett looked surprised. "I knew she could move her legs a little, but not her hand. Huh. . . . So, is that what she wanted — water?"

"I'm not sure. She drank some the first

time, but not the second," Melanie said. "I should have just asked her. Next time, I will."

"You mean like, 'blink once for yes, twice for no'?" he asked.

"Sure, why not?" Melanie said. "Don't you do that?"

"I've tried, but . . ." Garrett broke off and looked over Melanie's shoulder.

There was a low rumbling noise, and as Melanie turned to look, she saw Jeff's gardening truck lumbering toward them. Jeff stuck his head out the window as the truck rolled to a stop. "Car trouble?" he called out.

Melanie smiled and shook her head.

"What would you fix it with, anyway — a rake?" Garrett snapped.

Surprised, Melanie glanced at him, but all she saw was his back. Garrett was already walking to his car. He tossed the flowers onto the passenger seat, got in, jerked the car into gear, and sped backward down the drive toward the entrance.

Melanie couldn't see the red car anymore, but she could hear it idling. Every few seconds, Garrett revved the engine. It was a loud, impatient sound.

She looked at Jeff. Jeff shrugged. "He's definitely got an attitude," he said.

"I guess he's worried . . . about Lisa."

Jeff looked toward the end of the drive as Garrett revved his engine again. "Yeah," he said.

But he didn't sound as if he believed it.

Back in town, Melanie went into Fred's Diner for a cheeseburger. Trina Hodges was behind the counter, filling saltshakers and sugar bowls.

Trina was Melanie's age, and lived across the street from the Jacobs'. She talked a lot and laughed a lot. Melanie liked her, which was good, since she was the only young person she really knew so far.

"Mel!" Trina said as Melanie slid onto a stool at the counter.

"Hi, Trina. How was Texas?" Trina had been visiting relatives.

"Hot. The weather, I mean," Trina said. "The only guys I saw were cousins."

"So you didn't fall in love with a cowboy?"

"I wish." Trina laughed and straightened the red barrette in her short blond hair. "Listen, I talked to Fred about a job for you, but he's looking for somebody full-time." She rolled her blue eyes. "I'm lucky he didn't hire someone while I was gone."

"Well, thanks for asking, anyway," Melanie

said. "I guess I'll keep baby-sitting. And I got another part-time job this morning."

"Great!" Trina poured salt into a glass shaker. "What is it?"

"Reading to Lisa Randolph."

"You're kidding." Trina's blue eyes widened. "Isn't she still in the hospital?"

Melanie shook her head. "She's at home, in a wheelchair."

"Wow. I guess she came home while I was gone." Trina leaned her elbows on the counter. "Does she look really awful?"

"No," Melanie said. "I mean, she's got some bruises, and she can't move much, or talk. But she doesn't look gruesome or anything. She's pretty."

Trina shuddered. "Doesn't it make you feel kind of weird? Reading to her, I mean. I don't think I could stand it."

"It's the house I can't stand," Melanie said. "And the housekeeper. She's like an iceberg. I feel sorry for Lisa, being stuck in that place. You know her, don't you?"

"Sure." Trina got busy with the saltshakers again. "She hangs out — well, *hung* out — with another group. So we aren't close or anything, but I know her. She's kind of quiet, but friendly. And real smart."

"What happened to her?" Melanie asked. "Was she climbing the rocks or something? No, wait," she said. "First, I want a cheeseburger and a chocolate shake."

Trina gave the order to the cook, then poured coffee for a man who came in and sat at the other end of the counter. She fixed Melanie's shake and brought it to her, and by that time, the cheeseburger was ready.

"Now," Melanie said, pounding the bottom of the ketchup bottle. "What happened to Lisa? The housekeeper didn't even bother to tell me she was our age. I went there expecting somebody about eighty." She slapped the top of the bun back on her cheeseburger and took a big bite.

"Nobody knows exactly what Lisa was doing," Trina said, wiping away some salt she'd spilled. "It happened at night. In May, just before school was out."

"What was she doing out on those cliffs at night?"

Trina shook her head. "Maybe she went for a walk and slipped or something. Or maybe she was sleepwalking. Anyway, the lawn guy found her."

"The lawn guy?" Melanie said. "You mean Jeff Singer?"

"I think that's his name. Dark hair, cute? New here?" Trina said.

Melanie sipped her shake and nodded. "I talked to him this morning. But he didn't tell me he was the one who found Lisa." She wondered why.

"He probably wants to forget it," Trina said, shuddering again. "It must have been awfully gruesome. Her boyfriend was really broken up about it."

"Garrett Bailey? I met him this morning, too," Melanie said. She told Trina about the two near-collisions with him.

"But he was bringing Lisa flowers, so it was hard to stay mad at him."

"*That* definitely sounds like him. He was crazy about Lisa." Trina looked toward the door of the diner and added, "*Is*, I mean."

Melanie spun on her stool and saw that a group of kids — three guys and two girls — had just come in. The one in front was Garrett Bailey, still wearing his sunglasses. He was talking over his shoulder to one of the others, and Melanie couldn't make out what he was saying. But the sound of his voice was the same — tense and rapid, as if he couldn't get the words out fast enough.

Watching him, Trina murmured, "What happened to Lisa must have really changed him."

"What do you mean?"

Trina's pale eyebrows puckered in a frown. "I guess it made Garrett go a little crazy himself."

# Chapter 5

Still talking, Garrett looked around. When he saw Melanie, he smiled quickly and headed toward her.

"Hey, it's the reader!" he said, pushing the glasses up on his head as he walked. "And Trina."

"Hi, Garrett," Trina said, but Garrett didn't hear her. He was already talking to the group who'd followed him in.

"Neil, Kim, Heather, and Rich," he said, pointing them out as he said their names, "this is the girl I was telling you about. Melody."

"Melanie."

"Right. Melanie. Sorry," Garrett said. "Anyway, she's the one Sweet Georgia hired to read to Lisa. Melanie, these are some friends of mine and Lisa's." He started pointing again. "Neil, Kim — "

"You already did that, Garrett," the guy

named Neil said. He was as tall as Garrett, with sandy hair, a nice tan, and light-brown eyes that lit up when he looked at Melanie. Blond-haired Heather said hi. So did Rich; he looked like a football player by his size. Holding Neil's hand, Kim looked Melanie up and down. "You're new here, aren't you?" she asked.

Melanie nodded.

"She lives across the street from me," Trina said. "She's a senior, too."

"Well, welcome to the class," Neil said with a slow smile. His teeth were very white against his tan. "It'll be nice to have somebody new around."

Rich grinned. Heather rolled her eyes. Kim said, "I thought we came in here to eat."

"Food, right. That's exactly what we came in for," Garrett said. He straddled the stool next to Melanie and ordered a grilled cheese sandwich.

Neil sat down on Melanie's other side. There were three stools around the bend in the counter. Heather, Rich, and Kim took those.

Neil managed to sit with his shoulder touching Melanie's. Catching the look in Kim's eyes, Melanie leaned slightly away. These were people she'd be going to school with, and she didn't want to make any enemies if she didn't have to. She wasn't attracted to Neil, anyway. He was good-looking, but she didn't like the way he was flirting with her, not when it was so obvious that he and Kim were a couple.

Neil nudged Melanie slightly. "So, Melanie," he said, "Garrett told us you're reading to Lisa?"

"That's right." Melanie poked her straw around in her milkshake. "I hope it'll help."

"Help?" Garrett had been tapping his fingers on the counter to some beat in his head, but now he stopped. He narrowed his eyes at Melanie. "You think hearing a book'll help her walk and talk?" His voice was icy.

"Garrett," Heather murmured.

For a moment, Garrett kept looking at Melanie. His pale-blue eyes were sharp and angry. Then he seemed to give himself a mental shake. "Sorry," he said quickly. "This whole thing has kind of freaked me out."

Melanie hadn't left a boyfriend behind in Kansas. But she told herself that if she had, and if he'd fallen off a cliff and was paralyzed, *she'd* be freaked, too. "I didn't mean the reading would make her better," she said to Garrett. "I just meant it might help distract her . . . take her mind off things."

"Sure it will," Neil said smoothly. "What are you going to read?"

"*Jane Eyre.*"

"I thought you didn't want to bore her," Kim said.

"She was already reading it," Melanie said. "If she doesn't like it, I'm sure she'll figure out a way to tell me."

"Oh, sure," Kim said with a sneer. "In case you forgot, Lisa can't talk."

"Yeah, well, she's not a vegetable, you know," Melanie told her. "She *can* communicate."

"Oh, right, the hand thing!" Garrett looked up from the counter. "Melody — I mean Melanie said Lisa moved her hand this morning."

The others looked surprised. Why hadn't Lisa tried to communicate with them? Melanie wondered. What did they do when they visited her, sit in silence? "Did she like your flowers?" she asked Garrett.

"Yeah, I think so," he said. He seemed happier now. Not so tense. "She didn't move her hand or anything, but her eyes got real bright. She looked like she wanted to laugh." He smiled to himself, then at the others. "Remember her laugh?" he asked them.

"Yeah, it didn't go with the way she looked," Heather said. "She was quiet and serious-looking. And then somebody'd tell a joke or something, and out would come this great big laugh."

The rest of the group nodded, thinking about a Lisa Randolph that Melanie had never met. She felt like she was at a wake. *Lisa's not dead,* she wanted to tell them. *She's alive, and she's still the same person.*

Lisa was an outsider now, Melanie thought. She used to belong with these people. She used to fit in. Now she doesn't. Melanie knew how that felt.

When Trina arrived with the food, the others changed the subject — they talked about a rock concert they were trying to get tickets to, a new boat Neil's parents had bought, summer jobs. They all had part-time jobs, except for Garrett. He'd quit his when Lisa got hurt and hadn't found another one. Melanie got the feeling he didn't really want to.

Rich wasn't much of a talker, Melanie noticed, but Heather made up for it. Garrett ate fast, the way he seemed to do everything.

Neil didn't say much.

But he looked at Melanie — a lot.

Swiveling on his stool so he didn't have to turn his head to see her, Neil propped one elbow on the counter and smiled his slow smile every time she said something. Melanie felt like she was on display and it was starting to bug her.

It was bugging Kim, too. Melanie avoided looking at her, but she could feel Kim watching her and knew she was staring daggers.

Forget this, Melanie told herself. Just leave.

Wadding up her napkin, she put it on her empty plate and started to slide off the stool. Then she felt Neil's hand on her shoulder.

"Hey," he said. "If you need a ride or anything, I've got my car outside." His voice was soft, but not soft enough.

Lifting her head, Kim glared at both of them.

"Hey, what's the matter, Kim?" Neil sounded innocent. "I just asked if Melanie needed a ride."

His hand was still on her shoulder. Melanie shrugged it off and glanced at Trina, who rolled her eyes and went back to wiping the counter. Melanie picked up her bag. "Thanks, but I have a car," she said to Neil.

"See?" Neil said to Kim. "She said thanks. She's being polite, just like I was when I offered her a ride."

It was as if he wanted to get a rise out of Kim, Melanie thought. And it was working. Kim's high cheekbones were flushed and her dark eyes were snapping. But she still didn't say anything.

"Well, anyway, I guess you know how it feels now," Neil said to Kim. "You *do* remember what happened the last time somebody new came to town, don't you?"

Melanie was on her feet, ready to go. But Neil's words stopped her.

And so did the look on Kim's face.

It was shocked. Frightened. Frozen like a mask.

*Everyone* was frozen. Everyone looked as shocked and terrified as Kim.

No one said a word.

It was like the stunned silence of people staring in horror at a ticking bomb. They wanted to run. But they couldn't move.

Melanie felt chilled.

What did these people want to run from?

# Chapter 6

Garrett laughed suddenly, a little wildly. "Hey, Trina, what's going on here?" he said. "I mean, we come in all friendly and cheerful; we eat, and then wham! Total personality change! Does Fred put some secret ingredient in the food? And is there really a Fred, by the way?"

"The secret ingredient's hot pepper." Trina grinned. "But if I tell you about Fred, I'll get fired."

"I always suspected it," Garrett said. "There is no Fred. Just like there's no McDonald. No Denny. No Roy . . . wait. There *is* a Roy Rogers."

As Garrett talked, the rest of the group started to relax. Rich and Heather laughed. Neil walked around the counter to Kim and put his hand on her shoulder. Kim sighed, then half-frowned, half-smiled at him.

The frightened looks were gone. The stunned silence was over. Had she just imagined them? Melanie wondered.

But when the group left the diner, Kim shot Melanie a look of such dislike that Melanie felt chilled all over again.

*That* look was definitely real.

Melanie knew she had an enemy.

She turned to Trina, who was finished working for the day. "Want a ride home?"

"Great," Trina said. She pocketed her tips.

"Neil is so cheap," Trina complained as they left the diner and walked to Melanie's car. "His family's got tons of money and he leaves me a lousy quarter."

"He's cheap and a jerk," Melanie said. "I couldn't believe the way he acted."

"Kim'll get over it," Trina told her. "She and Neil fight all the time. Don't worry."

"I'm not worried about them, Trina," Melanie said as they got into the car. "I just don't like her blaming *me*. Did you see the way she looked at me when she left?"

"Yeah, but she'll get over that, too."

Melanie hoped so, but she didn't feel as sure as Trina. "What was Neil talking about, anyway?" she asked, backing out of the parking space. "Remember, when he told Kim that now she knew how it felt? And something about the last time somebody new came to town. Was he talking about Jeff?"

Trina shook her head. "No, I'm pretty sure he meant Peter."

"Who's Peter?"

"I can't remember his last name," Trina said, fiddling with the radio dial. "Norton or North or something. Anyway he was a college guy, backpacking around the country. He came to town . . . let's see, early in May, just before school was out for the summer." She found some music she liked, leaned her head back, closed her eyes, and continued the story. "I can still see him, walking into the diner with that stick."

"Stick?"

"Yeah, it was long and black, kind of like a cane but without the curve on top. A walking stick, I guess. The top of it was silver, shaped like a coiled snake." Trina laughed. "Anybody else would have looked really dumb with it, but he was the kind of guy who could pull it off."

"Cute, huh?"

"Dark, great build. Gorgeous."

The sun never made it out, and now it was

starting to sprinkle. Melanie set the wipers so they'd swoosh on every few seconds. "So?" she asked. "What happened?"

"Let's see. I'd just started working at Fred's, after school until seven," Trina said. "It was about four, I guess, and a lot of kids were in there. The group you just met, plus Lisa," she added. "Kim and Neil were arguing about something and the others were ignoring them. Then the door opened and Peter walked in."

"And?"

"And all the girls started drooling."

Melanie laughed. "You make him sound *unbelievable*."

"Well, he *was* good-looking," Trina said, opening her eyes. "But it wasn't just that. Maybe it was because he was somebody new and different, you know? He could have been a creep, I guess. But not knowing him, it was easy to imagine he was special and exciting."

The rain was coming down harder now, and Melanie turned the wipers on full speed.

"Where was I?" Trina asked.

"Drooling."

"Right, and Kim was the worst," Trina said, closing her eyes again. "Peter took a booth across from theirs, and Kim started talking to him, asking him questions about backpacking. Ha. The farthest Kim ever hiked is from her front door to her driveway."

"Neil got jealous, right?" Melanie said.

"Yeah. I think all the guys did, actually. Next to Peter, they probably felt about twelve," Trina said.

"Did he try to make them feel that way?" Melanie asked, fascinated by this boy she'd never seen. "I mean, did he flirt and egg the guys on?"

Trina shook her head. "Not really. Oh, he liked all the attention, you could tell. And he was friendly. But he was so smooth and sure of himself, he didn't have to flirt."

Melanie turned onto the street where she and Trina lived. "So when Neil was flirting with me, he was paying Kim back for Peter, huh?"

"Yeah. Pretty juvenile, I guess," Trina said. "But anyway, I don't think you have to worry about Kim splitting *your* lip."

Startled, Melanie looked over at her. "Splitting my lip? Are you kidding?"

"About Kim I am." Trina grinned. "See, Peter was going to stay Thursday and Friday night and leave on Saturday. He asked about places to camp around here, and then he left. When I saw him Friday afternoon, his lip was puffy and there was a scab on it."

"Neil punched him?"

"Well, Neil never came out and admitted it," Trina said. "But Heather told me that Neil and Rich and Garrett followed Peter after he left the diner. I don't mean they stalked him, or anything," she added. "They were just being dumb and macho and they told him he should take a hike. And Heather said Peter just laughed at them."

"Heather was there?"

"No, this is what Rich told her," Trina said. "And Neil was already steamed about Kim, so he hit Peter."

So *that's* what happened the last time somebody new came to town, Melanie thought.

It wasn't anything to brag about.

But it wasn't enough to make everyone freeze, the way they had in the diner.

Or had she imagined that moment? she wondered again.

No. It was real. Everyone had acted frightened.

But of what?

"Anyway," Trina went on, "Peter didn't leave. I know, because I saw him on Friday."

She sat up straighter as Melanie slowed for a stop sign. "And then I forgot all about him, because Saturday was the day Jeff found Lisa and nobody was talking about anything else."

"Did Jeff ever tell you about finding her?" Melanie asked.

"He never tells me anything," Trina said. "He says hi and stuff, but that's about it. Maybe he's shy, I don't know."

"He didn't seem shy to me," Melanie said. As she pulled into her driveway, she remembered the way Jeff had reached out and pulled a leaf from her hair. Definitely not shy, she thought.

But not totally open, either.

He'd clammed up when she'd asked what happened to Lisa. He'd drifted into his own thoughts for a minute, as if Melanie wasn't even there.

"I don't think he's shy," Melanie said. "I think he's private. Garrett doesn't like him," she added, and told Trina about Garrett's reaction on the driveway earlier. "You'd think he'd at least be grateful. I mean, if Jeff hadn't found Lisa, she might have died."

"Yeah, well, like I said, Garrett's gone a little crazy since Lisa fell." Trina took hold of the door handle. "But maybe he has a good reason not to like Jeff."

"Like what?"

Trina shrugged. "You said it — Jeff's private. Maybe he's hiding something. And maybe Garrett knows what it is."

*In her dream that night, Melanie was driving through a thick, swirling mass of fog that her headlights couldn't pierce. Somehow, she knew she was driving up the cliff road. She was afraid she'd miss a turn and plunge off the edge. The windows were closed, but the fog seeped in anyway. It drifted through the car and wrapped itself around her face until she couldn't see at all.*

*Suddenly, like magic, the fog was gone.*

*Jeff was standing there.*

*In one hand he held a sign that said "Private." In the other was a black walking stick with a coiled silver snake on top. He waved the stick like a traffic cop, urging Melanie to drive forward.*

*Straight ahead was the edge of the cliff.*

*Jeff smiled. His dark eyes glittered. Attractive. Dangerous. He waved the stick again.*

*And Melanie put her foot down on the gas pedal.*

As the car started to go over, she shot straight up in bed.

Gasping, Melanie put her hand to her chest. Her heart was racing.

It was only a dream, she told herself. Forget it. Jeff's not dangerous.

Melanie looked around. Her dog, Oliver, was curled up near her feet, as usual. She reached down to pat him and realized that the room was so bright she was squinting. For the first time in what seemed like weeks, the sun was out.

Nobody was home, she discovered when she went downstairs. A note on the refrigerator told her that her mother was looking at possible places to rent for her vet's office, and that her father was at a school-board meeting.

Melanie let the dog into the backyard, ate a muffin, showered, and dressed. She played with Ollie outside for a while, then went in and listened to some music until her mother came back. After lunch, Melanie got in the car and drove toward the cliff road and the Randolph house.

She thought the sun would have changed the look of the house somehow. Made it brighter or more welcoming. But it still seemed like a prison to her. If anything, the sun made it seem more foreboding.

The gardening truck was parked in the same

place as the day before. Melanie got out and looked around. But except for the black-and-white cat dozing on the terrace wall, the grounds were empty.

Suddenly, the image from her dream came back.

Jeff, waving a silver-topped walking stick.

Waving her over the cliff to her death.

She shook her head. She was letting this place upset her, that was all.

As Melanie headed up the walk, Georgia Hudson opened the door and waited for her. "It's a great day, isn't it?" Melanie said. "And it's really warm. I was thinking maybe I could read to Lisa on the terrace."

The housekeeper hesitated, then shook her head. "Not today. Maybe another time. Lisa's tired."

She didn't look tired, Melanie thought as she walked into the library. Lisa's chair was facing the door this time, and she looked fine. The bruise on her cheek had faded some more, and her eyes were wide and bright. She was dressed in pale-green today, and someone had braided her hair. Melanie wondered who. Somehow, she couldn't imagine Georgia Hudson doing it.

"I'll leave you alone," Ms. Hudson said from

the doorway. "If you need anything, the intercom's always on. All you have to do is speak up." She glanced at Lisa and pulled the door shut behind her.

Melanie pulled the ottoman across the room again, then turned Lisa's chair so it faced the windows. "You ought to be able to see your cat, and the sunshine out there," she said.

*Jane Eyre* was on the table where Melanie had left it. As Melanie picked it up, she said, "By the way, I met some of your friends yesterday. Garrett and Rich, Neil, Heather, and Kim." She decided not to say what she thought of them all. "And Trina Hodges," she added. "I live across the street from her. A re-cap will probably bore you so I'll just start where I left off."

Melanie sat down and started to suggest a signal for Lisa to use to communicate with her. Blinking for yes and no, like Garrett had said. Or the hand movement. But Lisa's eyes were already fastened on the book. What clearer signal could there be? Melanie started reading.

The next chapter was about the return of Mr. Rochester and his guests, including the beautiful and snotty Miss Ingram, who made nasty remarks about governesses and looked at Jane as if she were a toad.

Melanie stopped reading and said, "Rochester's planning to marry this gem. No wonder Jane gets depressed. She's only the governess, and she's in love with him, but she won't admit it to herself. I guess that's one thing that makes this book old-fashioned. *We'd* admit it — at least to ourselves — wouldn't we? And we'd definitely tell Rochester he was acting like a dork."

Lisa kept her eyes on the book, but Melanie thought she saw them crinkle at the corners.

Melanie grinned and went on reading as Jane talked about how she'd stopped seeing Rochester's bad points. " *. . . that something which used to make me fear and shrink, as if I had been wandering amongst volcanic-looking hills, and had suddenly felt the ground quiver, and seen it gape.*"

Melanie stopped. Lisa's hand had moved up, then down to the arm of the chair . . . again. This time the movement was faster and stranger. It *had* to mean something. But what?

Melanie glanced at the camera, then said, "I hope this doesn't seem silly to you, but maybe we could work out some kind of signal together. So when I ask you something, you can tell me yes or no." She glanced at the camera again. Maybe Ms. Hudson wasn't watching. Maybe she was on the phone and not listening. "Why don't you blink once for yes and twice for no," Melanie said. "Do you want some water?"

Lisa's eyes stayed on the book. She didn't blink.

Melanie sat back. She was *sure* Lisa understood. Maybe she just didn't want to communicate right now. "I'll just keep reading," she said, and found her place.

The next time Lisa moved her hand, Melanie was reading Jane's description of a new arrival at Thornfield Hall. " . . . *the driver rang the doorbell, and a gentleman alighted, attired in travelling garb; but it was not Mr. Rochester; it was a tall, fashionable-looking man, a stranger.*"

Two pages later, Lisa lifted her hand a third time, as Melanie read, *"I was now able to concentrate my attention on the group by the fire, and I presently gathered that the newcomer was called Mr. Mason."*

Melanie stopped. She didn't know what it meant. She knew Lisa must have a reason for doing this. But when she'd suggested a signal, all Lisa did was stare at the book.

*All Lisa did was stare at the book,* Melanie thought. Just like she was doing now.

Melanie looked down at the last words she'd read, then back at Lisa.

*A message.* Lisa's using the *book* to try to tell me something.

And as if Lisa had read her mind, she slowly raised her eyes from the book to Melanie's face. Then she blinked.

Once for yes.

# Chapter 7

"A message?" Garrett shoved his dark glasses up and gave Melanie a doubtful look. "Don't you think there are easier ways of doing that, even for somebody like Lisa?"

The two of them, along with Neil and Kim, were in the back parking area near the garages. Melanie hadn't had a chance to test her theory that Lisa was trying to tell her something. Just as she'd been about to, Ms. Hudson had come into the library, told her she'd been reading for an hour and that she could go.

But Melanie was almost positive she was right. And when she'd seen Garrett and the others roar up the drive in Garrett's red car, she'd waited to tell them. She was sure Garrett, at least, would be as excited as she was. Instead, he looked skeptical.

"It's probably just a coincidence," he said.

"I don't think so," Melanie said. "I mean,

the only time she moves her hand is when I'm reading something."

"Maybe she's bored. Maybe the message is 'stop,' " Kim said coldly. "Did you ever think of that?"

"No, Kim," Melanie said. "I'm sure *you'd* be bored, but Lisa definitely isn't."

Kim shot her a dirty look. Melanie ignored it and turned back to Garrett.

Garrett was staring at her. "I've seen Lisa every day since she came home," he said. "Sometimes two or three times a day. I talk to her, I tell jokes, I sing, I do everything but stand on my head. No, wait — I think I did stand on my head once." He took a step toward Melanie. "Lisa and I have been together a long time. If she had something to say, she'd say it to *me*."

"But . . ."

"And no offense, Mel," Garrett went on, "but I don't think you ought to mess around and play guessing games with Lisa."

Garrett's message was perfectly clear: *Back off*.

But why? Melanie wondered. Was he just being protective?

Melanie didn't know. She thought Garrett was wrong about Lisa — she didn't need protecting, she didn't need someone to stand on his head. She needed someone to *listen*. But Melanie decided not to argue. "Is that another present?" she asked, pointing to a small white box he was carrying.

"Huh? Oh, yeah," he said. "It's a necklace, a gold chain with a heart."

Kim took the box and opened it. "Hey, it's just like the one you gave her last year, when you started going together," she said. "What happened to that one, anyway?"

Garrett didn't answer. He was staring toward the end of the yard, where the lawn met the forest.

Jeff Singer was there. He was moving along the edge of the yard, carrying a pair of long-bladed clippers.

"I don't know what happened to it," Garrett said. He kept his eyes on Jeff. "When I gave it to Lisa, she said she'd never take it off. And she didn't. She wore it all the time."

Remembering the thin red line around Lisa's neck, Melanie shivered. The necklace must have caught on something when she fell, slicing into the skin until the chain finally broke.

"Hey, what am I doing?" Garrett said suddenly. "My girl's waiting. See you, Mel. And be careful when you leave — that drive's pretty narrow." Laughing, he started up the walk toward the house.

Kim followed after Garrett, but Neil didn't move. He was watching Melanie. Not again, she thought with a sigh. "Aren't you going to see Lisa?" she asked.

"In a second," he said. "I wanted to talk to you first."

Melanie shifted her weight and looked at her watch. Maybe he'd take the hint.

"It won't take long." Neil moved closer to her. "It's about yesterday, at the diner," he said quietly. "I wanted to apologize. I know I embarrassed you, but I wasn't trying to." He smiled his slow, easy smile. "I hope you won't hold it against me."

This guy was really something, Melanie thought. He wasn't trying to embarrass *her*, just his girlfriend. The girlfriend who was standing on the walk right this minute, watching them together and ready to explode.

Melanie had had enough. "Look, Neil," she said. "I don't know what kind of game you're playing, but just leave me out of it, okay? And if you really want to apologize to somebody, try Kim."

Melanie stepped around him and walked toward her car, hoping he wouldn't follow. When she looked back, Neil was ambling up the walk. Kim hadn't waited for him, though. She was just going inside, and as Melanie watched, she slammed the door in Neil's face.

But not before she gave Melanie another acid look.

Forget about her, she told herself. She's obviously warped. She should be mad at her boyfriend, not me.

But she could still feel the hatred in that look.

Jeff walked up to her.

Melanie asked, "So, are you finished for the day? I thought you'd be busy pulling down those killer vines."

"I was going to, but Ms. Hudson told me to put it off. She said something about not disturbing Lisa." Jeff's eyes narrowed as he glanced at the terrace. "I'm pretty sure that wasn't the real reason, though," he said under his breath.

He was tense again. Angry. "What do you mean?" Melanie asked.

"I mean she wants me to stay away from . . ." Jeff stopped. "Hey, never mind that," he said quickly. "Since we're both through for the day, how about getting something to eat?"

He moved closer, carrying the sharp-bladed clippers in one hand.

He smiled, and his dark-brown eyes sparkled.

Suddenly, Melanie remembered what she'd felt in her dream.

A sense of excitement.

And of danger.

"Melanie?"

She blinked.

Jeff was staring at her curiously.

Melanie took a deep breath. "Sure," she said. "I'd love to get something to eat."

Jeff's smile widened.

Melanie felt as if she were right at the edge of the cliff.

Ten minutes later, she was sitting at a booth in Fred's Diner, talking to Trina and waiting for Jeff, who'd gone home to take a quick shower.

"I happen to know you're the first girl Jeff's asked out since he moved here, Mel," Trina said excitedly. She glanced over her shoulder to make sure she wasn't needed behind the counter yet. "How did you manage to get a date with him?"

"I didn't *manage* it," Melanie said. "He just asked me if I wanted to get something to eat. Maybe I looked hungry," she added dryly.

"Well, whatever," Trina said. "But listen, if you learn any secrets, you have to promise to tell me."

"Secrets?"

"Jeff's secrets," Trina said. "He's Mr. Mysterious, remember?" She looked over as the door opened. "Here he is!" she hissed.

As Trina sped back toward the counter, she stopped and spoke to Jeff, then waved dramatically to where Melanie was sitting.

"Hi," Jeff said, sliding into the booth across from Melanie. He was in fresh jeans and a light-blue T-shirt. His dark hair was still damp from the shower and he smelled of soap. "Trina told me to tell you not to leave until you talk to her. She said it was really important."

She wants to pump me about Jeff, Melanie thought, frowning. She liked Trina, but she was awfully nosy. No way would Melanie tell any of Jeff's secrets, even if he told them to her.

She wished Trina hadn't even mentioned the word. Was it some secret that made Jeff so exciting . . . and scary?

"Hey, is something wrong?" Jeff asked.

Melanie shook her head. "Nothing except I'm hungry," she said. "Let's eat."

When the food came, they talked about the usual things. Where they'd moved from. What they liked and didn't like. Where they wanted to go to college. There was nothing scary or exciting about any of it, and Melanie started to relax.

Jeff had moved from Illinois, he told her. He was crazy about basketball and history.

"Not horticulture?" Melanie asked.

Jeff laughed. "I don't think so, but it's a good job, actually. I was lucky to get it. And I like being outside."

"Especially today, I bet," Melanie said. "I tried to talk Ms. Hudson into letting me read to Lisa on the terrace this afternoon, but she didn't like the idea. She said Lisa was tired."

"Was she?"

"I didn't think so. Anyway, being on the terrace wouldn't exactly wear her out." Melanie drank some soda. "I know Lisa's friends come visit her," she said. "And I guess Ms. Hudson's responsible for her most of the time, so she has to be careful. But I get the feeling everybody treats Lisa like she's . . . not really there. Or not really part of things. And I know how that feels." She smiled at him. "I guess you do, too, right? Being new here."

Jeff nodded. "But it doesn't really bother me."

"Well, it bothers me," Melanie said. "And I'll bet it bothers Lisa, too. I think she's trying to tell me something. Maybe not about that, but . . ."

"Trying to tell you something?" Jeff broke in. He looked startled. "You mean she tried to talk?"

Melanie shook her head. Then she explained what had happened when she was reading *Jane Eyre*. "She tapped the chair yesterday, too," she said. "Ms. Hudson told me to give her some water. And I guess I was too busy worrying about myself — you know, how I sounded and whether I was being watched on the monitor — to pay any attention." She leaned her elbows on the table. "But today, I didn't do that. I tried to get Lisa to work out some kind of signal with me — blinking for yes and no."

Jeff was leaning on the table, too, his face only a foot from Melanie's. He looked interested. Very interested. "Did it work?"

"I didn't think so," Melanie said. "Then I got the idea that she was trying to use the *book* to say something. Because she tapped when I was reading certain things. And just when I thought that, she blinked." She sat back. "But then Ms. Hudson came in, so I didn't get the chance to ask Lisa if I was right. I will tomorrow, though."

"When did she tap the chair?" Jeff asked. "I mean, what words?"

"I don't know if it was a word, or a sentence, or a paragraph, or what," Melanie said. "I don't remember what I was reading every time she did it, either. I'll have to go back and check in the book."

Jeff stared at her for a moment. Finally, he said, "Let me know if you figure it out, will you? I'd like to know what Lisa has to say."

"Sure." Melanie finished her Coke. "Did you know her before she fell?"

He shook his head. "I'd seen her at school and I'd just started working on the grounds at her house," he said. "I think we'd said hi to each other about two times. Why?"

"I just wondered, that's all." Melanie hesitated. "Trina told me you found her," she said.

He stared at her again, and now he looked angry. "And you want the gory details?"

"No!" Melanie said. What was the matter with him? "I just . . . forget it. Forget I even mentioned it."

"No, that's okay, Melanie. Sorry. I didn't mean to snap at you." With a sigh, Jeff slumped back against the booth. "It was about eight in the morning," he said. "I was working on the far side of the house, where the cliff cuts in all the way back into the woods. It was windy the night before. There were branches all over."

He sounds so cold, Melanie thought. So remote. As if he's talking about something that didn't really happen to him.

"I was cleaning the branches up when I saw that black and white cat climb up over the edge of the cliff. I don't know why I walked over and looked down, but I did. And I saw Lisa. She wasn't moving. I called out, but she didn't answer. I climbed a little way down, and I called out again. She mumbled something."

He stopped, as if he were listening to Lisa's voice, trying to understand what she'd said. "Then I realized I couldn't do anything by myself and I might fall, too. So I ran to the house and got help."

Melanie waited.

But Jeff's face had closed up, the way it had yesterday.

There was more to the story. Melanie had no idea what. But she knew there was more.

She also knew she wasn't going to find out from Jeff. He'd said all he was going to say.

But he hadn't told her everything.

Maybe Trina was right. Maybe Jeff Singer *did* have a secret.

At home later, Melanie tried to put the thought of Jeff's secret out of her mind.

He's exciting, she told herself. He's different. You like being with him. That's all you need to know.

Standing in her living room, Melanie looked at all the unpacked cardboard boxes lining the walls. Most of them were full of books, which couldn't be shelved because the shelves hadn't been built yet.

One of the boxes held her copy of *Jane Eyre*. After digging through eight boxes, Melanie finally found the book and took it up to her room. Oliver followed and curled on the bed with her while she paged through it, trying to find the parts where Lisa had tapped the arm of her wheelchair.

She'd tapped in five places that Melanie could remember. The first one was when Jane saved Rochester from being burned. The second was a description of Blanche Ingram. The third was when Jane told how she'd stopped noticing Rochester's bad points. The last two were about the new man who came to Thornfield Hall.

Actually, she couldn't be completely sure that Lisa had meant to tap in those exact places. Maybe it was hard for her to lift her hand. Maybe she was trying to do it a few sentences earlier, or even a paragraph.

Melanie stuck Post-Its on the pages and

shut the book. She'd ask Lisa tomorrow.

Lisa had something to say, and Melanie was going to help her say it.

With the sun out for a second day in a row, Melanie thought for sure she could get Lisa onto the terrace. But as soon as she stepped inside the Randolph house, Ms. Hudson nodded toward the library. Then she hurried away before Melanie could say a word.

Looking down the hall, Melanie saw Lisa's father waiting outside the housekeeper's office. He had a sheaf of papers in one hand and a small suitcase at his feet. He'd obviously come back from his trip, but it looked like he'd be leaving again soon.

Mr. Randolph and Georgia Hudson went into the office and shut the door.

Melanie wondered if the two of them had something going. None of your business, she thought. Anyway, they were in the office with the monitor. And even if they didn't watch it, they'd be able to hear whatever Melanie said. Suddenly, she felt very self-conscious about asking Lisa about her "message."

"Hi, Lisa," she said, walking into the library. "Hey, you're wearing Garrett's necklace. It looks beautiful."

Lisa stayed still.

Melanie dragged the ottoman across the floor again. At least nobody kept putting *Jane Eyre* back on the shelf. It was exactly where she'd left it, on a low table near the rear windows.

She picked it up and opened it to her place as she walked back to the ottoman. As she did, something slipped out and drifted to the floor at her feet.

It was a small piece of white paper, folded in half. Melanie bent and picked it up. Moving toward the ottoman again, she opened it.

And then she stopped moving.

Her scalp prickled and her mouth went dry. She felt the blood drumming in her ears.

The paper held a single sentence, written in crooked block letters: *If you want to keep reading, be careful who you talk to.*

It was a message. A message for Melanie.

But it wasn't from Lisa.

# Chapter 8

Lisa was watching her. There was a questioning look in her gold-flecked eyes.

Melanie's hand was shaking. Quickly, she crumpled the note and stuck it in the pocket of her shorts.

"Just a scrap of paper," she said. Her voice was shaky, too. She forced a smile, but her face felt stiff.

It had to be Kim.

Just yesterday, she'd watched from the sidewalk while Neil flirted with Melanie for the second day in a row.

There'd been hate in Kim's eyes. Melanie had seen it and felt it. And there was hate in the note.

"Is there a problem, Melanie?" Georgia Hudson's crisp voice came over the intercom.

"No!" Melanie looked at the camera and quickly smiled. "No problem!"

No problem except Kim. And wondering what that hatred would make her do next.

The note in her pocket made a crinkling sound as Melanie sat down on the ottoman. Her fingers felt as stiff as her face, and she fumbled with the pages of the book. Finally she found the place where she thought Lisa had moved her hand yesterday.

"Remember where I left off?" she asked. "Somebody new just came to Thornfield Hall: *'I was now able to concentrate my attention on the group by the fire, and I presently gathered that the newcomer was called Mr. Mason.'* "

Melanie stopped to take a breath, her eyes on Lisa's face. Lisa parted her lips slightly. Her eyes were on Melanie's.

It was a small movement, but it was deliberate. Melanie was sure of it — Lisa was trying to say something. If only she didn't have an audience watching and listening from another room, she'd tell Lisa she *knew* she was trying to tell her something. Then they could work out a way for Melanie to understand the message.

For now, Melanie just said, "Right. That was the place." Then she went on reading.

The reading helped. She didn't forget about the note, but she was able to shove it into a corner of her mind.

Melanie read carefully, pausing every few sentences to make sure she didn't miss any movement of Lisa's hand or eyes. But there wasn't any. Lisa was as still as she'd been the first time Melanie saw her.

When she reached the end of the chapter, she stood up and stretched. As she did, she looked out the rear windows and saw five people heading up the flagstone walk toward the back door.

One of them was Kim.

"You've got company," she said to Lisa. "Garrett, Neil, Heather, Rich . . . , and Kim."

"It hasn't been an hour yet," Georgia Hudson said over the intercom. "I'll tell them to wait in another room until you're finished."

Good, Melanie thought. She didn't feel like meeting Kim face-to-face yet.

As she started to sit down, she noticed Jeff striding across the lawn toward the terrace. He waved when he saw her, and pointed to the rear windows. Then he put both hands on his throat in a comic strangling gesture. He was obviously going to attack the vines.

Melanie smiled and waved back. "Okay, chapter twenty," she said to Lisa, scanning the first few sentences. "Oh, good, this one's really spooky."

The chapter started out with Jane Eyre getting out of bed to pull her curtain because the moon was so bright it kept her awake. Just as she did, she heard a horrible savage cry that made her blood run cold.

" *. . . I now heard a struggle,*" Melanie read, "*a deadly one it seemed from the noise; and a half-smothered voice shouted —*

" *'Help! Help! Help!' three times . . .*"

Melanie looked over and suddenly stopped short.

Lisa had moved. Not her hand this time. Just her forefinger, raised and then lowered.

Just to be sure, Melanie backtracked. When she read *"Help! Help! Help!"* Lisa lifted her finger again.

The movement was tiny. No one else could possibly have seen it. The only reason Melanie did was because she'd been watching so carefully for *something*.

Remembering how many people might be watching on monitors, Melanie decided not to get into a guessing game right now. But she gave Lisa a curious look. She obviously wanted Melanie's help to say something. But why was she making her gesture so *small*?

"Melanie?" It was Georgia Hudson again. "Mr. Randolph has to leave town and he's coming in to say good-bye to Lisa. And then her friends are waiting to see her. Maybe this would be a good time to stop after all. There isn't much time left, anyway."

Melanie was impatient to keep reading, but she didn't have much choice. "Sure," she said, closing the book and standing up. "I'll see you tomorrow, Lisa."

Lisa's eyebrows came together in a slight frown.

Mr. Randolph came in as Melanie was heading for the door. "Keep up the good work, Miss . . . uh . . ." he smiled quickly and hurried across the room.

Pulling the door shut behind her, Melanie turned around and saw Garrett coming out of another room. As he headed toward her, she looked past his shoulder.

"Are you waiting for somebody else?" he asked, looking behind him.

"No, I want to get out of here before I run into Kim. I don't want to see her," Melanie told him.

Quickly, Melanie headed down the hall toward the back door. Garrett came after her.

"What do you have against Kim?" he asked, shoving his dark glasses up on his head.

"I didn't have anything against her until today." Melanie pushed open the door and they stepped outside. "But she's got something against me." Melanie had been shocked when she saw the note. Shocked and a little scared. But now she was furious. "Kim left me a message in the book I was reading yesterday, telling me to keep away from Neil."

"You're kidding." Garrett's pale-blue eyes widened. "She said that?"

"Well, not in so many words." Melanie turned to face him. "But that was the idea of it."

"Huh!" Garrett leaned against the low stone wall, looking confused. Then he shrugged. "Oh, well. Don't let it bug you. Hey, listen, Mel," he said, "I think I'd better apologize again."

"For what?" Melanie looked toward the garages, but Garrett's car blocked hers from view. "Don't tell me you hit my car."

"*Moi?* A reckless driver?" Garrett raised his eyebrows. "No, it's nothing like that, I promise. I was thinking about what you said yesterday. About Lisa maybe trying to tell you something?"

Melanie nodded.

"When you told me, I guess . . . well, I was a little jealous, I think," Garrett said. "I mean, I wish *I* was the one, you know? So when I told you not to play guessing games with her, I must have come off sounding like her bodyguard or something."

"Yeah, you did," Melanie said.

Garrett ducked his head, looking slightly embarrassed. "Well, anyway, I was watching you read today. There's a monitor in just about every room — did Sweet Georgia tell you about them?"

"Oh, yes," Melanie said. "I feel like I'm onstage."

"Right. So, the thing is, I could tell Lisa was listening real hard. And I was thinking . . . maybe you're right. Maybe she *does* want to say something. And since you're the one who's reading, it makes sense that she's trying with you."

"Now if I can just figure out what it is," Melanie said. "She moved her hand on the word *help*."

"Help?" Garrett said, looking startled and worried. "But she's okay. I mean, not okay, but she's got all the help anybody can give her. Wait a sec — you think she's in pain or something?"

"No, I think she's just asking for *my* help," Melanie told him. "You know, to say whatever it is she's trying to say."

"Oh, right! Sure, that's it," Garrett said. "I should have figured that out."

"The other place was something about a bunch of people around a fire, and a newcomer called Mason." Melanie shook her head. "That doesn't make any sense to me. Does it to you?"

"Somebody named Mason?"

"Right. And a fire. Some people around a fire."

Garrett shook his head, his face blank.

"Well, anyway, I'll keep working on it," Melanie said.

"Good. Great."

"And if I ever do figure it out, I'll let you know. Unless it's — " Melanie stopped suddenly.

"Unless it's what?" Garrett asked.

*Private,* Melanie thought.

Maybe what Lisa wanted to say *was* private.

First, Lisa had used her whole hand to signal. Today, she'd just used her finger.

Lisa had to know about the cameras and the monitors. She knew people were watching her almost every minute.

She'd taken a chance and used her whole hand, until she was sure Melanie had figured out what she was trying to do. And then she'd signaled with her finger. She'd made the gesture so small Melanie wouldn't have seen it if she hadn't been looking for it.

Why?

Because people were watching.

Because she didn't want anyone else to know.

Lisa was hiding something. And she was trusting Melanie — a perfect stranger — to figure out what it was.

But why? Why wouldn't she tell someone she knew?

Melanie felt her mouth go dry again.

Because Lisa was terrified.

# Chapter 9

"Melanie?"

She jumped. Garrett was watching her. If Lisa didn't trust him, Melanie couldn't either.

"What's up?" he asked. "You drifted away in the middle of a sentence."

"Did I? Sorry." An airplane was droning overhead and Melanie pointed to it. "I heard the plane and started thinking about my parents," she said quickly. "They left for vacation this morning."

"And they didn't take you? Too bad." Garrett grinned and started to say something else. But then he noticed Jeff walking toward them from the terrace, and his grin faded quickly. He flipped his sunglasses back down and waited until Jeff got closer. "Are you about finished on the terrace?" he asked sharply.

Jeff ignored him and looked at Melanie. "Hi," he said.

"Hi." Melanie could feel the tension running between them like a current.

"Exactly how long do you plan to spend hanging around those windows?" Garrett asked. He took a step toward Jeff.

Jeff raised his hands. For a second, Melanie thought he was going to take a swing at Garrett.

Instead, Jeff pulled off his thick work gloves. "As long as it takes to rip the vines down," he said.

"Right." Garrett smiled without any humor. "Kind of convenient, isn't it? I mean, you must get a real good view of everything in the library. See anything you like?" he asked with a sneer.

Jeff stared at him for a second, and Melanie saw his jaw tighten. Garrett glanced at Melanie. "See you," he said abruptly, and went back into the house.

Melanie suddenly realized she'd been holding her breath. She let it out in a rush. "What was that all about?"

Jeff stared at the closed door of the house, slapping the work gloves against his thigh. "How'd the reading go?" he asked, ignoring her question. "Did you figure out what Lisa's trying to say?"

"Not yet," Melanie said impatiently. "What's going on between you and Garrett?"

"Why don't you ask him? I'm sure he'd be glad to tell you." Jeff stuck the gloves in the back pocket of his jeans. "Do you like to bowl?"

"What?" Melanie shook her head at the change of subject. "What's bowling got to do with Garrett?"

"Nothing. Let's forget about Garrett." He moved closer to her, smiling. "Because if you like to bowl, maybe you'll go with me tonight."

Melanie felt herself smiling back. He was so changeable. Maybe that was part of his attraction.

"Is that a yes?" Jeff asked.

"That's a yes," Melanie said. She told him where she lived, and watched him for a second as he walked back to the terrace.

He *was* mysterious, like Trina said. But he could also be very warm. He was *definitely* keeping something to himself.

He'd tell you if he wanted to, she thought. You've got Lisa to worry about. That's enough.

"Are you sure this is from Kim?" Trina asked, looking at the note Melanie had found in *Jane Eyre*.

"Who else?" Melanie took the piece of paper back, tore it into little pieces, and dropped them on the picnic table.

Trina wasn't working today, and the two of them were on the patio behind Melanie's house, drinking Cokes and talking.

"Kim hates me," Melanie said, watching Oliver dig around in the backyard. "Never mind that it's all Neil's fault. She thinks I'm after him."

"I guess you're right." Trina stretched out on the redwood bench. " *'If you want to keep reading, be careful who you talk to.'* What's she saying — if you keep talking to Neil, she'll scratch your eyes out?" She laughed. "That is so dumb!"

"Dumb? It's sick," Melanie said. "How come she and Lisa are such good friends, anyway? I thought Lisa was supposed to be nice."

"She is. And I don't think she and Kim are that close," Trina said. "Kim hangs out with them because of Neil, and Neil's pretty good friends with Garrett." She sat up suddenly. "Maybe Garrett wrote the note."

"Garrett?" Melanie frowned.

"Well, you said he was jealous because Lisa's trying to tell *you* something and not him," Trina said. "Maybe he put it in the book yesterday. Later he might have decided it was really stupid, which it is, but he didn't get a chance to take it out before you saw it."

Maybe, Melanie thought. Lisa didn't seem to trust Garrett. But why would Garrett care who Melanie talked to? "I still think it's Kim," she said.

"You're probably right." Trina took the Frisbee Oliver had unearthed and tossed it back into the yard for him. "Well, anyway, now that Kim's got it out of her nasty little system, she'll probably leave you alone."

Melanie picked up the little scraps of paper and let them drift through her fingers.

She hoped Trina was right.

After Trina left, Melanie took a shower and put out jeans and an orange tank top to wear later. Wrapped in a short terry-cloth robe, she went to the kitchen and ate a cheese sandwich. Oliver padded after her and lay on her feet while she ate. When she went back to her room, he followed. He wanted company, she guessed, and she was glad, because the house was empty and quiet. Her parents wouldn't be back for ten days.

Stretching across her bed, Melanie leafed through her copy of *Jane Eyre*, reading the pages she'd stuck Post-Its on. She got a pad of paper, wrote them out in order, and tried to make some sense out of them.

Something about a plot.

Somebody with large black eyes.

Something that scared Jane, as if she'd been wandering in volcanic hills.

A stranger arriving at Thornfield Hall.

A group of people by the fireplace, and the stranger named Mason.

Help.

Melanie frowned. Was Lisa trying to tell her about a plot? A stranger who'd frightened her and plotted something? A stranger with large black eyes?

Who was a stranger to Lisa?

Melanie's heart started to hammer.

Jeff Singer. Jeff Singer was a stranger to Lisa. His eyes were big. They weren't black but they were such a dark brown, they might as well be.

And Jeff Singer had a secret.

He hadn't told Melanie everything about the morning he'd found Lisa. She knew that. What had he left out?

He'd asked her to let him know when she figured out what Lisa was trying to tell her. He was really interested in it. Too interested.

Lisa had something to say — something she was afraid to tell anyone but Melanie. And Jeff

Singer wanted to know what it was. Jeff Singer, the stranger.

The phone rang suddenly, and Melanie jumped. Oliver charged down the hall into her parents' room where the upstairs phone was. He didn't stop barking until Melanie picked it up. "Hello?"

Static.

Melanie said hello again. She thought she heard a voice, very faint and far away. "David, is that you?" she said, thinking it might be her brother, calling from some Italian village in the Alps. "David?"

Nothing.

Melanie hung up. The clock on the dresser said six-thirty. Jeff would be here soon. Was he the stranger? If so, what was Lisa trying to tell her about him?

Get a grip, Melanie, she told herself. You're not even completely sure Lisa's afraid of *any-body*. And if she is, it doesn't have to be Jeff.

The phone rang again. Melanie grabbed it before the dog finished his first bark.

This time it was the neighbor down the street, asking if Melanie could baby-sit to-morrow night. She said yes.

Back in her room, Melanie got dressed. Then she brushed her hair and teeth and went downstairs to wait for Jeff. She was in the kitchen, putting out fresh water for the dog when the phone rang a third time.

"Ollie, hush!" she said. The dog ignored her, dancing around her feet, trying to attack the wall phone. Melanie almost tripped over him before she managed to pick it up. "Hello?"

Static again.

But it wasn't static, Melanie suddenly realized. It was a crackling sound, but more like paper or plastic. "Hello?" she said again.

This time, someone answered.

"Melanie," a voice said. It was a high, thin, breathy voice, almost like one of the little girls she sat for.

"Cassie, is that you?" Melanie asked. "Does your mom know you're on the phone?"

"I know you got my message, Melanie," the voice said. "I hope you'll pay attention."

Melanie gasped.

The voice had changed.

It wasn't high and breathy anymore. It was deep and gutteral.

It sounded almost inhuman.

# Chapter 10

With a cry, Melanie dropped the phone. It clattered against the wall and swung wildly back and forth. The dog barked and snarled at it so loudly Melanie almost screamed. She grabbed the phone and hung it up.

Her hands were sweaty. Her pulse was racing. Suddenly, she spun around.

She knew it was crazy, but she half-expected to see a face outside the patio door, peering in at her. But not a twisted, ugly, monster face, like the voice on the phone.

A face that was all too human.

Kim's face.

Because it had to be Kim. She obviously *hadn't* gotten it out of her nasty little system. Sick little system was more like it, Melanie thought with a shudder.

It would almost be better if the caller had

been someone totally anonymous, some sicko who liked scaring people for kicks. Knowing who it was made it much too personal.

Even though it was still light outside, Melanie lowered the blind over the patio doors.

Leaving the kitchen, Melanie went through the rest of the house, closing curtains and blinds and turning on lamps. She didn't want to come into a dark, empty home later. Oliver would be here, but Oliver only attacked noises, not people.

In the upstairs hall, Melanie stopped, breathing hard.

If Kim could see you now, she'd be laughing, she thought.

She'd love to see you racing around with shaky hands and sweaty hair.

She *wants* you frightened.

Don't let her do this to you.

Melanie forced herself to take a deep breath. Then another. Her hands were clenched into fists and she opened them.

She was still unnerved. But she was starting to get mad, too.

Stomping back downstairs, she flipped on the porch light. At the same moment, the doorbell rang.

Furious now, Melanie yanked open the door.

Jeff Singer was standing on the porch.

Jeff Singer, with eyes such a dark brown they were almost black. Jeff, the stranger.

I could be completely wrong, Melanie thought, staring at him. Lisa's message could change tomorrow. And tonight, Melanie didn't want to be alone. *Couldn't* be alone.

Shaking away thoughts of a dark-eyed stranger, Melanie grabbed her jacket from the coat tree. Then she stepped outside and slammed the door shut behind her.

"What, no introductions?" Jeff asked.

"You want to meet my dog?"

"Well, I like animals, but I was thinking of your mom or dad, actually."

"They're out of town." Melanie twisted the door handle, making sure it was locked. "I am really glad to be out of that house," she said.

Jeff looked at her. "Are you okay, Melanie?"

For a second, she was tempted to tell him about Kim. But only for a second. She didn't want to talk about it. She wanted to forget it. "I'm fine. With my parents gone, the house is kind of quiet, that's all," she said. "I'm ready for some noise."

He smiled. "You'll get plenty of that at a bowling alley."

"Then let's go," she said.

Pretending that Kim's head was on top of one of the bowling pins improved Melanie's aim and got rid of most of her anger. By the end of the second game, she was ahead of Jeff.

"I'm thinking of asking for a handicap," he said, peering over her shoulder as she wrote down her score. "A couple of strikes, maybe?"

"Forget it," Melanie said. She was very conscious of how close his face was to hers. If she turned her head just a fraction of an inch, she'd be kissing him.

"Okay." Jeff rested a hand on her shoulder. "How about something to drink?"

"Sure. A Coke." His hand was warm. "You're just trying to break my streak, though, and it won't work," she said.

"We'll see." He squeezed her shoulder and headed for the concession stand.

Melanie sat down on the molded plastic bench to wait. She could still feel the heat from Jeff's hand on her skin.

She didn't want him to be the stranger.

Leaning her head back, Melanie listened to the rumble of bowling balls and the clatter of pins. When she opened her eyes again, she saw Heather and Rich standing by the bench next to hers.

"Hi." Heather smiled a little uncertainly. "Melanie, right?"

"Yes. Hi."

Rich gave Melanie a lopsided grin and went off to rent shoes.

As Heather sat down, Melanie looked past her toward the concession stand. There was a long line. She couldn't see Jeff. "Are you guys alone?" Melanie asked, hoping that Kim and Neil weren't somewhere around.

Heather nodded. "Why?"

It *was* a strange question, Melanie realized. "I just wondered," she said lamely. She also suddenly wondered if Heather knew what Kim had been doing. But Heather seemed friendly enough.

"I wanted to go to the movies," Heather said. "Rich wanted to bowl. We flipped a coin." She flicked a strand of blond hair out of her eyes and glanced at Melanie. "I heard you reading to Lisa today. How can you do it?" she asked with a shudder.

"What do you mean?"

"Isn't it kind of . . . well, creepy? Sitting there with her for so long?" Heather shuddered. "I mean, when I fix her hair or just go visit her, I can hardly wait to leave. It's awful, I guess, but I can't help it. She just sits there. It's like I don't know her anymore."

No wonder Lisa wasn't trying to communicate with her own friends, Melanie thought.

"My mom's the one who made me volunteer to do her hair," Heather went on. "I know I shouldn't mind, but I wish somebody else would do it. I mean, Georgia Hudson lives right there in the house."

"She doesn't seem like the type," Melanie said.

"Right." Heather snorted. "Personally, I think she's after Mr. Randolph. He's got tons of money. She guards that house as if it's hers, even though she only started working there a couple of weeks before Lisa fell."

So, in a way, Georgia Hudson was a stranger, too. She'd only been with the Randolphs a few weeks.

If there *was* a stranger plotting something, maybe it was Georgia Hudson, with her hooded dark eyes.

It could be Georgia Hudson instead of Jeff.

Melanie glanced toward the concession stand again. It was still packed. She still couldn't see Jeff.

Heather followed her gaze. "Oh, there's Rich," she said. "I guess he's getting us something to drink." She turned back to Melanie. "Who did you come with?"

"Jeff Singer."

"Oh, the new guy?" Heather wiggled her eyebrows up and down. "He's good-looking." She paused. "I just hope Garrett's wrong about him."

Melanie's stomach knotted. She knew she was about to hear something she didn't want to.

"Wrong?" she asked. "What do you mean?"

"Well," Heather said, stretching her legs out in front of her. "Garrett thinks Jeff stole a necklace from Lisa. He thinks Jeff did it when he found her, right before he went and got help."

A shiver ran down Melanie's spine.

It couldn't be true!

"Maybe . . ." Melanie stopped and swallowed. "Maybe it fell off when she fell."

Heather shook her head. "Garrett says no. He actually climbed down and looked for it. He told Ms. Hudson about it, too, and now she's always keeping her eye on Jeff," she added.

So that's what Garrett meant about looking

in the library windows, Melanie thought. He thought Jeff was a thief?

Is that what Lisa thought? Was that what she was trying to tell Melanie?

"The necklace is definitely missing," Heather went on. "Garrett's not making that part up. But personally, I think he's jealous."

"Of Jeff?" Melanie sounded surprised. "Jeff told me he hardly knew Lisa."

But maybe he'd lied about it, Melanie thought.

"I'm pretty sure Garrett's mad because Jeff found her," Heather said. "Garrett's crazy about Lisa. I just know he wishes he was the one who rescued her."

Just like he wanted to be the one she was trying to tell something to, Melanie thought. Still, there was a big difference between being jealous and lying.

Unless it wasn't a lie. Melanie's mind was swimming in circles.

"You know what I think?" Heather cut into Melanie's thoughts. "If the necklace got stolen, I'll bet it was somebody else who took it. See, a couple of days before Lisa fell, this backpacker came into — "

"I know," Melanie broke in. "Trina told me all about him. Peter something."

"Oh, that's right. I told her," Heather said. "So you know what Neil did, huh?"

"Split his lip."

"Yes, and Garrett and Rich just let him." Heather shook her head in disgust. "Anyway," she went on, "when Lisa found out, she was really mad. And she told Peter he could camp on her property. The woods go on for miles behind the house and the Randolphs own it all."

"Did he camp there?"

"I think so. Lisa told everybody he was going to, anyway," Heather said. "None of the guys liked that idea. But we just thought they were being macho and jealous. Maybe we were wrong. Maybe Peter was a thief. Gorgeous — but a thief."

So maybe the backpacker was the stranger, *not* Jeff, Melanie thought hopefully. If he'd stolen Lisa's necklace, maybe that's what Lisa was trying to say. He could have sneaked into the house and Lisa saw him, chased him, and fell. And he kept going.

Melanie asked suddenly, "What color were Peter's eyes?"

"I'm not sure." Heather squinted, as if the backpacker were standing at the other end of the bowling alley and she couldn't see him very well. "His hair was real dark. His eyes were brown, maybe. Or gray." She paused. "Or they could have been blue."

Or green or hazel, Melanie thought. She'd have to ask Trina.

But no matter what color his eyes were, the backpacker had been camping somewhere in the woods. It didn't make sense to sneak into the house just for a necklace. And how did that thin red line get around Lisa's neck? He couldn't have walked in and ripped the necklace off without Lisa screaming.

Jeff could *still* be the stranger. But it could also be Georgia Hudson. Or somebody else she didn't even know about.

Melanie shook her head. Nobody knew . . . except Lisa.

Rich came back then, with bowling shoes and sodas. Heather sighed and put the shoes on. Melanie looked for Jeff again and finally saw him. He was coming from the direction of the main doors, carrying two cans of soda.

"I waited fifteen minutes and then the concession stand was out of Coke," he said. He set the cans down and ran a hand over his windblown hair. "So I went to the little grocery store across the street."

He picked up one of the cans and held it out to Melanie.

Melanie stared at his hand.

She saw it reaching for a thin gold chain, and twisting it. Twisting it so tight, it cut into Lisa Randolph's flesh.

"Melanie?"

She blinked the image away and reached for the can.

Her fingers touched Jeff's.

And she shivered again.

"So what happened to your winning streak?" Jeff teased as he drove her home later. "Did my ploy really work? Making you wait broke your concentration?"

"I guess so," Melanie said, laughing. It wasn't true, of course. She just hadn't been able to stop thinking about what Heather had told her. That's what had broken her concentration.

She looked over at Jeff. He was watching the road, whistling under his breath.

"What are you thinking about?" Jeff asked.

Tell him, she thought. Let him deny it.

"Um . . . something Heather told me," Melanie said nervously. She took a deep breath. "She told me why Garrett doesn't like you."

Jeff was silent.

"Look, I can understand why you didn't tell me about it," Melanie said quickly. "It must be awful, having somebody accuse you of something like that and not being able to prove him wrong."

Jeff still didn't say anything.

Melanie forced herself to go on. "Maybe Garrett's just upset," she said. "He wanted to be the one to rescue Lisa. He feels the same way about me," she added. "He wants to be the one Lisa is trying to talk to. Or he did, anyway. He apologized."

"You think he'll apologize to me, too?" His voice was cold. Icy.

Melanie didn't answer.

Jeff pulled into Melanie's driveway and shut the engine off. Silently, they got out of the car and went up the front walk.

"Listen," Melanie said when they were on the porch. "I'm sorry I brought it up. I just . . ."

"You just wanted to hear me say I didn't do it," Jeff interrupted quietly. His voice was warm again.

He leaned close. Melanie's heart started

hammering and she almost backed away.

But Jeff was smiling now. A little scary. But very sexy.

He leaned closer. "I didn't take Lisa's necklace," he whispered.

He brushed his lips against hers, then turned and walked back to his car.

He denied it, Melanie thought as she watched him go.

But did she believe him?

The dog started barking the minute Melanie put her key in the lock. He quieted down when she came in, then raced into the kitchen and waited for her to let him out.

Shrugging off her jacket, Melanie tossed it on the kitchen table and went to raise the bamboo blind that covered the sliding glass doors. She gripped the strings and tugged. The blind started rolling up from the bottom.

There was something red on the glass.

It hadn't been there earlier.

Melanie frowned and kept pulling. When the blind was almost at the top, she froze.

She was looking at words. Words written in block letters, just like the ones on the note.

But these letters were big. They covered both doors, and were written in red. A dark, glistening red.

Bloodred.

BE CAREFUL, MELANIE, the bloodred words said. I KNOW WHAT YOU'RE DOING.

# Chapter 11

Melanie stared in horror at the ugly words.

Was Kim really that desperate?

And if she was, what would she do next?

Suddenly, it struck her: Someone had been *here, in her house*. While she was out, somebody had come in and scrawled a bloodred threat across her door.

Terror flashed through her. Letting go of the blind, she raced out of the kitchen and up the stairs.

Tearing through the house, gasping for breath, Melanie looked in closets and behind doors and under beds.

The house was empty. Kim hadn't done anything else.

Yet.

Back in the kitchen, her heart still pounding, Melanie stood in front of the patio doors. . . .

She couldn't see the words anymore, but she didn't have to.

She'd never forget them.

Something cold and wet touched her hand. Melanie jumped and spun around.

Just the dog, wanting to go out.

She looked at the blind again. They're just words, she told herself. Sick and crazy, but just words.

Melanie raised the blind again. Her fingers fumbled with the lock, but she finally got it to work. She slid the door open just enough for the dog to slip through.

And then she remembered: She'd locked the doors before she left. The front door was locked when she got home and so was this one.

So how did Kim get in?

Slowly, Melanie raised her hand and rubbed a finger across one of the letters. Nothing came off. She licked her finger and rubbed again. Nothing.

Reaching through the opening in the door, she rubbed the outside of the glass. The letter smeared, leaving something sticky on her finger.

Red nail polish.

Kim had just been in the backyard, not in

the house. She'd written the message so it looked like it was on the inside. But she'd never been inside.

Knowing that made Melanie feel better. But not safe. Not completely safe.

Because she didn't know what Kim's next move would be. This was more than just a joke. Melanie wondered how far Kim was willing to go.

The next morning it took Melanie a good half hour to get the nail polish off the glass. She still felt paranoid, wondering what Kim might be planning for her. But she was also feeling angry. The harder she cleaned, the angrier she got.

By the time she was done, she was furious.

She called Trina, but Trina was at the diner. She'd switched shifts with someone else for the day. It was eleven-thirty. Melanie decided to eat at Fred's, hang out and talk to Trina, then go to the Randolphs'. She got her marked-up copy of *Jane Eyre* and left the house.

"What's the matter with you? You look kind of weird," Trina said when Melanie sat down at the counter. "It can't be the food, you haven't eaten yet, ha-ha." She peered more closely at Melanie's face. "Oh. I guess I shouldn't be joking. Was the date with Jeff that bad?"

"No," Melanie said. "It was okay."

"Just okay?"

Melanie didn't want to talk about the date. She had more important things to talk about. She ordered a hamburger and waited until Trina brought it. Then she told her about the phone call and the bloody-looking message.

"You're kidding. No, I know you're not," Trina said quickly. "But, I mean, this is weird."

"Weird? It's sick, Trina. I mean, I thought she'd been in my house! And next time, she just might be!"

"Listen, you've got to talk to her," Trina said. "You probably should have done it right after you got that note."

"I don't want to talk to her," Melanie said, moving the pickle to the edge of her plate. "But I guess you're right. I don't know what to say, though."

"Well, you can start with hi." Trina tilted her head toward the door.

Turning, Melanie saw Kim.

She was at the cashier's and it looked like she was ordering something to take out.

She was alone.

Melanie took a sip of water, a deep breath,

and slid off the stool. She felt her anger building again as she crossed the floor. By the time she reached Kim, she didn't bother saying hi.

"I've gotten all three of your messages, Kim," she said. "Maybe you'd like to tell me why you're sending them to me and not to Neil. And maybe you'd like to tell me to my face this time."

Kim frowned and eyed Melanie as if she were a strange microscopic specimen. "Maybe *you'd* like to tell me *what* you're talking about," she said coolly.

Turning her back on Melanie, Kim walked a few feet to where there were several plastic chairs for take-out customers. She sat down in one and pulled a stick of gum out of her pocket.

Melanie followed and stood in front of her. "Okay, Kim," she said. "Here's what I'm talking about. Somebody's really mad at me. So mad, they left a note in the book I'm reading to Lisa, telling me if I want to keep reading, I'd better be careful who I talk to. Then they called me on the phone with a warning. And then, they left a message at my house. On the patio doors. In nail polish. Red nail polish, like blood."

Kim folded the gum into her mouth and started chewing. "Too bad," she said.

"Look, I know you're mad because Neil's been flirting with me," Melanie told her.

"Yeah? So?"

"So be mad at *him*, not *me*."

"What makes you think I'm not mad at him?"

"I'm sure you are," Melanie said. "But I'm telling you I'm not interested in him. And I think you already know that, so I really don't appreciate it when you take it out on me."

"You think I should take it out on him?" Kim asked.

"Do whatever you want," Melanie said. "Just leave me out of it."

Kim's order came then, and she got up to pay for it. Before she left, she stopped in front of Melanie. "Not that it's any of your business, but I did take it out on Neil," she said. She smiled coldly. "I broke up with him."

Great, Melanie thought. Kim probably blamed her for that, too.

"And by the way, I didn't send you any messages, Melanie," Kim said. "I don't care how much you read or who you talk to. It sounds like *some*body does, though." She smiled again. "So maybe you'd better take their advice, and be careful." Kim slammed the door as she left.

What had Kim said? *It sounds like somebody cares how much you read and who you talk to.*

And the note in the book: *If you want to keep on reading, be careful who you talk to.*

Someone wanted her to keep her mouth shut about any message from Lisa.

"Well, what happened?" Trina asked.

Melanie looked at her. Could she trust her? Trina didn't know that Lisa was trying to say something. Melanie hadn't told her. Trina couldn't be the one.

"Listen," Melanie said. "I need to talk to you, but it's private and it's serious. You can't tell anybody! You have to promise!"

"Okay, okay, I promise." Trina leaned on the counter, looking curious. "What is it?"

"Lisa's trying to tell me something," Melanie said. "Something she doesn't want anybody else to know."

"What does that have to do with Kim?"

"I'm starting to think it doesn't have anything to do with her," Melanie said. She told Trina everything that happened so far. Then she pulled out her copy of *Jane Eyre* and read the quotes that Lisa had tapped on.

"No wonder you're spooked," Trina said when Melanie had finished. "But Mel, are you sure? I mean . . ."

"You mean am I sure I'm not imagining it?" Melanie asked hotly. "You saw the note I got in the book. If I imagined that, then so did you.

But it was real. So was the voice on the phone and the letters on the door."

"I know, I know," Trina interrupted. "But listen — it could *still* be Kim. Do you really believe she didn't do it just because she said she didn't? You know . . . maybe Garrett sent the messages."

"I don't know what to believe."

Melanie suddenly remembered something. "What color were Peter's eyes?"

"The backpacker?" Trina thought a second. "Um . . . brown, maybe?"

Melanie sighed. Maybe she was getting closer to some answers.

"Wait a minute," Trina said. "You think he might be this stranger?"

"I don't know. I'm just trying to figure it out," Melanie said.

"But you don't even know what Lisa's trying to tell you yet," Trina said.

"I know," Melanie groaned. "This is all too much for me! I'll just have to keep on reading."

"Be careful," Trina said.

Driving up the cliff road later, Melanie turned the radio on loud, trying to blast the confused thoughts out of her head. It didn't work.

As she turned onto the Randolph property, the music ended and the weather report came on. The sunshine break was over. It would be back to fog and rain for at least five days.

Melanie couldn't wait five days. She had to get Lisa out onto the terrace where she could talk to her, ask her questions. And she had to do it today.

As she stopped next to Jeff's gardening truck, she shivered slightly, remembering his lips on hers.

Stop it, Melanie told herself. He could be the one. He left you alone at the bowling alley while he went across the street for Coke. Or so he said.

But he could have gone to your house and painted a bloodred message on your door.

As she walked to the back door, Melanie looked at the terrace. It was empty. The vines were all down, as far as she could tell, and Jeff wasn't around.

Georgia Hudson greeted her at the door, as usual. This time, she walked with her into the library.

Was she suspicious or was she just doing her job?

Lisa was in her usual place. Waiting.

Waiting to tell her secret.

"Here she is, Lisa," Ms. Hudson said in her obnoxiously sweet voice. She turned to Melanie. "I'll be in my office."

Sure, Melanie thought. In her office listening and watching. "Ms. Hudson?" she said. "I heard the weather report while I was driving up here, and today's the last sunny day we're going to have for awhile." She looked at Lisa. "So this'll be Lisa's last chance to get out in the sun, at least for five or six days. I think she'd like it, don't you?"

Georgia Hudson looked toward the windows. She started to say something, but she was interrupted by a humming sound. It was a low hum, but in the quiet library it seemed loud.

It was coming from Lisa.

As soon as the housekeeper looked at her, Lisa stopped humming. Her bright eyes shifted to the windows, then to Melanie, then back to the windows.

It was obvious. Lisa wanted to go outside.

Ms. Hudson frowned. But she nodded. "All right," she said. "I don't suppose there's any harm in it."

"Great," Melanie said. "The windows open, don't they? I'll help you."

Once the windows were open, Ms. Hudson went behind Lisa's wheelchair, and pushed it out onto the terrace. She positioned Lisa so she was shaded by a big branch that hung over the edge of the roof.

"It is nice out here," she said, looking at the sky.

Just don't decide to join us, Melanie pleaded silently.

"A little cool, though," Ms. Hudson went on. "It never really gets hot in this part of the country. I suppose I'd better get something for Lisa's shoulders." She went back into the house.

Melanie didn't think Lisa needed anything for her shoulders, but she was glad the house-keeper was gone. Sitting on the low wall, she faced Lisa. "As soon as Ms. Hudson brings your sweater or whatever," she said, "and goes back inside, then we can talk. You *are* trying to tell me something, aren't you?"

Lisa's eyes closed and quickly opened.

"Good, at least I know I'm not imagining it." Melanie glanced at the windows to make sure the housekeeper wasn't coming back yet. "I have all kinds of questions, but I'll wait. I know you don't want anyone else listening."

Lisa blinked again.

Melanie started to say something more, but she stopped. Lisa was making the low hum-ming sound again, her eyes looking toward the steps. The black and white cat appeared and was creeping carefully toward the wheelchair. He sniffed the footrest, then leaped onto Lisa's legs and sniffed her face and hair. Then he turned around a couple of times and settled himself on her lap.

Lisa looked back at Melanie.

"I brought my own book today," Melanie said. "I marked all the places in it where you moved your hand. I could go back and ask you questions about them, or I could keep reading. Do you want me to . . . ? Wait a minute. Where is it?"

Melanie looked around. She didn't have the book with her. "Sorry, I left it in the car. It'll just take me a second to get it."

Hopping down from the wall, Melanie left the terrace and walked across the lawn to her car. The book was on the front seat. She picked it up and had just slammed the door when she heard a car roaring down the drive. Garrett, she thought.

And then she heard another sound, one that drowned out everything else.

It was the shrieking, teeth-rattling sound of a chain saw.

The cat shot into the air and was halfway across the terrace before its feet hit the ground.

Melanie couldn't see the chain saw, but she didn't have to. She knew who was using it.

And when she looked, she knew what he was using it on.

It was the tree branch, the one that hung over the roof edge and shaded part of the terrace. The branch was almost as thick as a person's body. Melanie could see it shake and quiver as the saw bit into it.

Jeff Singer was up on the roof, out of sight, slicing into the branch. Melanie couldn't hear the creaking sound the branch was making. She didn't need to.

She could see what was happening, all too clearly.

The thick, heavy branch was about to fall.

And it was about to fall on Lisa.

# Chapter 12

The branch jerked and dropped lower.

In another few seconds, it would break free completely.

Melanie was already halfway across the lawn, screaming at Jeff to stop. It was useless. Jeff couldn't hear her over the sound of the saw. Nobody could hear her.

The lawn seemed as wide as a football field. Melanie knew she was running fast, but it felt like she was moving in slow motion.

Finally, she reached the terrace. She bounded up the steps and tripped, scraping her knee on the rough stone. Jumping up, she raced along the terrace and around to the back of the wheelchair.

She gripped the rubber-covered handles and shoved.

The chair didn't move.

She shoved again. This time it lurched forward. But not nearly enough.

Why wouldn't the stupid thing move?

Frantic, Melanie looked down to see if there was a rock or something blocking the wheels. And finally, she saw the lever on the side. A brake. Ms. Hudson had put on the brake.

Trying not to think about the heavy branch swaying overhead, Melanie fumbled with the lever and released the brake.

She gripped the handles again and pushed hard, shoving the chair as fast as she could.

Garrett was running toward them now, his mouth open, shouting. Georgia Hudson was in the open windows, holding something yellow in her hands.

When she reached the end of the terrace, Melanie stopped and turned.

The branch jerked again and dipped lower. Even over the roar of the saw, Melanie could hear the shriek of the splintering wood.

The branch dipped and shrieked one last time, then crashed to the stone floor of the terrace. It bounced when it hit, scattering leaves and dust and pieces of bark.

The saw rumbled like a car engine revving at a stoplight.

Then, suddenly, everything was quiet.

Melanie put her arms around herself to try to stop trembling.

Before Melanie could catch her breath, Garrett and Ms. Hudson were at Lisa's side.

"Lisa, are you all right?" Garret shouted.

"What happened?" Georgia Hudson demanded, staring at the fallen branch but not at Lisa.

Melanie wanted to tell Garrett to stop shouting. Obviously Lisa was all right. And she felt like telling Ms. Hudson to use her eyes and figure it out herself.

But before she could say anything, Jeff Singer walked around the corner of the house with a chain saw in his hand.

Garrett flew at him. "You stupid jerk!" he yelled. He jabbed his fingertips against Jeff's chest. "What do you think you were doing? Look at that branch — if it had hit her it could have killed her!"

Garrett kept jabbing with his fingers, forcing Jeff to step backward. "What's the matter with you? Didn't you even look before you started with that saw? Didn't you even think to warn anybody?"

In a lightning-quick motion, Jeff stuck out his free hand and grabbed Garrett's wrist.

From where she was standing, Melanie

could see Jeff's eyes. They were narrowed in anger, and darker than ever.

Jeff didn't say anything, he just looked at Garrett for a moment. Then he dropped Garrett's hand and looked at Melanie and Lisa and Ms. Hudson. "I'm sorry," he said. "I was up on a ladder against the tree trunk. The tree's around the corner of the house, so I couldn't see onto the terrace." He put the saw down and stepped up to the fallen branch. "Garrett's right — I should have called down before I started. I'm glad no one was hurt."

"You're *lucky* no one was hurt," Garrett said.

Jeff ignored him and grabbed hold of the thick end of the branch. "I'll get this branch out of the way."

"He's fired, right?" Garrett said to Ms. Hudson. "I mean, you're not letting him get away with such a dumb move, are you?"

Georgia Hudson finally came to life. "Calm down, Garrett," she said. "I'll handle this." She draped a yellow shawl over Lisa's shoulders and wheeled her toward the open French doors. "I'll speak to you in a few minutes, Jeff." She pushed the wheelchair inside and shut the windows.

Jeff had the branch off the terrace now and

he dragged it around the corner of the house. He was back in seconds. Without another word, he picked up the saw and walked across the lawn toward his truck.

Garrett stood with his hands on his hips, watching Jeff walk away. "Can you believe that guy?" he said to Melanie. "Sweet Georgia better fire him, that's all I've got to say."

Melanie wondered if she would. According to Heather, Ms. Hudson didn't trust Jeff. What just happened with the branch would be the perfect excuse to get rid of him.

Melanie started to go inside with Lisa, but Garrett's next words stopped her.

"I thought it was an accident," he said. "Now I'm beginning to wonder."

Melanie had already thought of that, the minute she heard the saw. But it didn't make sense. "How could it not be an accident?" she said. "If you're going to chop a branch down on somebody, you don't give them a warning."

"He didn't give a warning."

"Yes, he did," Melanie said. "With the chain saw. That's a pretty loud warning if you ask me."

"What are you doing, defending him?" Garrett said. "Oh, right, I guess you are. I heard you went out with the guy."

Melanie frowned. "What does that have to do with anything?"

"I just wondered how well you really know him, that's all."

Melanie didn't want to hear this. Not from Garrett. "I know what you think about Jeff," she said. "That he took Lisa's necklace. And now you think he deliberately tried to hit her with a tree branch." She crossed her arms. "But I don't know you any better than I know Jeff," she added. "So why should I believe *you*?"

Garrett lifted his sunglasses and stared at her. "Good point," he said with a little laugh.

Melanie was mad, and still shaken by what had just happened. And she remembered what Trina had said — that Garrett could have sent her those messages.

"What are you doing here, anyway?" she asked. "You ought to know by now that this is when I read to Lisa. How come you always show up when I'm ready to read?"

Garrett laughed again. "What are you trying to say?"

"That maybe you're still jealous because Lisa's trying to tell *me* things instead of you," Melanie said. "And maybe *you* sent me that note. *And* called me on the phone *and* wrote on my door. To scare me and get me to stop reading to her."

"Hold it a second," Garrett said, shaking his head. "You told me about some note you got. You said Kim wrote it."

"I thought she did."

"And now you think *I* did?" he asked. "And you think I called you and . . . what? . . . wrote something on your door?" He shook his head again as if there were a gnat buzzing around his ears. "You're not making any sense. I admitted I was a little jealous when you told me about Lisa and the book. But scare you? That's crazy."

His blue eyes were wide and he looked completely baffled. Either he was telling the truth, or he was a great actor.

Melanie looked toward the parking area by the garages. Jeff was standing by his truck, and Ms. Hudson was talking to him.

Maybe it *was* Ms. Hudson, Melanie thought again. She could be after Mr. Randolph. Maybe she was trying to get Lisa out of the way so she and Mr. Randolph could be alone. And Lisa knew it and was trying to tell Melanie.

It was hard to see Georgia Hudson actually writing a message in nail polish, though. But she could have hired someone to do it.

Melanie's thoughts were interrupted by

Garrett's talking. "What?" she said.

"I said if someone doesn't want you reading to Lisa, maybe you ought to take another look at your gardener friend." Garrett jerked his chin toward Jeff. "You know what you said about the chain saw being a warning?"

Melanie nodded.

"Lisa was the only one on the terrace then, remember?" Garrett said. "Jeff could have seen her there, alone. So even though she heard the saw, there wasn't a thing she could do about it. And he knew it."

"Dropping a branch on someone because of a stolen necklace is a pretty drastic thing to do, Garrett."

"Yeah, it is," Garrett agreed. "But maybe it's not just the necklace he wants her to keep quiet about."

Melanie looked across the lawn at Jeff again. Garrett's jealous of him, she thought. And he thinks Jeff stole the necklace.

Maybe Jeff did.

But what happened with the branch was an accident.

Wasn't it?

When Melanie went inside, Lisa raised her eyebrows in a questioning look.

Probably wondering what Garrett and I

were talking about, Melanie thought. She would have told Lisa, except Georgia Hudson was back in the house, listening. And who knew where Garrett was? Or Jeff.

"I guess we'll be reading inside today after all," Melanie said. "It would've been nice to be out in the sun, but we'll do okay without it." She meant, *you can still signal me while I read. I'll figure it out somehow.*

Lisa hummed softly for a couple of seconds.

Melanie picked up Lisa's copy of *Jane Eyre.* She must have dropped hers when she was running toward the terrace before. It didn't matter. She wouldn't be reading the quotes and asking about them, like she'd planned.

Melanie found the place where she'd left off. "Okay. Jane heard a horrible cry, and then a big struggle going on in the room above hers. And then she heard somebody yell 'Help, help, help!' "

Lisa lifted her finger from the arm of the wheelchair.

"Right. There were guests at Thornfield, including the obnoxious Miss Ingram. They all heard the cry for help and came running out of their rooms to see what was going on.

"Jane left her room, too, and saw everybody dashing up and down the hall, calling for Mr. Rochester.

*"And the door at the end of the gallery opened, and Mr. Rochester advanced with a candle;"* Melanie read, *"he had just descended from the upper story. One of the ladies ran to him directly; she seized his arm: it was Miss Ingram.*

*" 'What awful event has taken place?' " said she. " 'Speak . . .' "*

Pretending to pause for breath, Melanie nodded at Lisa. Lisa had just raised her finger on the line: *"What awful event has taken place?"*

Then Lisa signaled Melanie on the line: *"And dangerous he looked; his black eyes darted sparks."*

Melanie read three more sentences. Then she stopped again. But not because Lisa had raised her finger.

Something about Lisa's last signal reminded her of something . . . of what? She couldn't remember. She shook her head and went on reading.

Melanie paused again, still thinking about that last signal. Rochester looked dangerous, and his eyes darted sparks. She kept coming back to it, like a dream she knew she'd had but couldn't remember.

What did it remind her of?

Lisa was watching, her eyebrows raised again.

Questioning what Melanie was thinking.

But Melanie couldn't tell her. She bent her head to the book and went on reading.

In the middle of Jane's description of how quiet Thornfield Hall got after all the commotion, Melanie stopped a third time.

She'd finally remembered.

Jane Eyre was talking about Edward Rochester.

But Melanie was thinking of Jeff Singer.

She was thinking of the way his eyes looked when Garrett was yelling at him.

Narrowed to slits, furious, and darker than ever.

*"And dangerous he looked; his black eyes darted sparks."*

# Chapter 13

Garrett was right.

Lisa was alone when Jeff started sawing.

Jeff said he couldn't see down onto the terrace. But he could have heard Melanie talking to Lisa.

And then, Melanie had left to get her book. Jeff would have heard her say it.

Lisa was alone, and Jeff knew it.

And he made his move.

Melanie looked at the new gold heart around Lisa's neck. Jeff wouldn't have taken such a terrible chance because of a gold necklace, would he?

But Garrett said he might have something else to hide.

Another secret. Worse than a stolen necklace. A secret he was desperate to keep.

But what?

A low humming sound broke into Melanie's

thoughts. She looked at Lisa. The humming stopped.

Lisa's eyes, still questioning, shifted from Melanie's face to the book.

Melanie took a deep breath and let it out. "Sorry," she said. "I was thinking about something." She bent her head to the book again and found her place.

Thornfield Hall was quiet now. No more savage cries. Melanie read of how Jane waited, knowing that Rochester would come for her help. When he did, he led her up to the third floor of the house, and into a room where a man sat in an easy chair next to a bed.

*"Mr. Rochester held the candle over him; I recognized in his pale and seemingly lifeless face — the stranger, Mason: I saw — "*

Lisa moved her finger. Melanie nodded and went on reading.

Rochester left, saying he'd be back and telling Jane not to speak to the man. Through another door, Jane could hear someone groaning, laughing, and sometimes making horrible, gutteral animal sounds.

Jane was scared, but she waited, thinking. *"What crime was this, that lived — "*

Lisa lifted her finger.

What crime was this? Melanie wondered

with a shiver. She had to keep reading. *"What mystery, that broke out, now in fire and now in blood, at the deadest hours of the night?"*

Lisa signaled again.

*"And this man I bent over — "* Melanie read a few sentences later — *"this common-place, quiet stranger — how had he become involved in the web of horror? and why had the Fury flown at him?"*

Lisa's finger moved.

A web of horror, Melanie thought. She and Lisa were tangled in one together.

Lisa signaled a fifth time on the line, *"He moaned so, and looked so weak, wild, and lost, and I feared he was dying; and I might not even speak to him!"*

Melanie made herself keep reading and watching for Lisa's signal. But the phrases kept swirling in her head — crime, fire, and blood, a web of horror. She couldn't stop thinking of Jeff Singer and his dark, angry eyes.

Outside, Melanie took a deep breath and looked around. The cat was stalking something in the grass. The sky was still blue, but she could see clouds forming in the west. Garrett's red car was still parked near hers.

Jeff's truck was gone.

When Melanie got to her car, she saw her copy of *Jane Eyre* on the driver's seat. She picked it up and got in.

Then she stared at the book. How did it get back in the car?

She'd had it in her hand when she heard the saw. Then she started running to the terrace. She must have dropped the book somewhere along the way.

Somebody put it back.

Georgia Hudson? Garrett? Jeff?

One of them had looked at it. One of them had seen all the Post-Its Melanie had stuck inside, and all the brackets she'd put around the lines Lisa had signaled on.

One of them had as much chance now as Melanie did of figuring out what Lisa was trying to say.

Whoever it was didn't even need to know which lines Lisa had signaled on today. Because that person already knew the whole story. And that person didn't want Melanie to figure out the ending.

Georgia Hudson, Garrett, or Jeff.

Melanie couldn't trust any of them.

The phone was ringing as Melanie unlocked the front door. Inside, Melanie hurried toward the kitchen.

She stopped suddenly in the doorway.

What if it was the same caller as before?

Melanie could hear the voice in her mind. Gutteral. Menacing. Almost inhuman.

What would it say this time?

The phone rang again. The dog barked at it and looked at Melanie. She opened the patio door and shooed him out.

The phone kept ringing.

Pick it up, she told herself. Get it over with.

She grabbed the phone, cutting it off in the middle of a ring.

It was Jeff Singer.

"Hi." Melanie's voice sounded strange to her, sort of phony-bright, the way Georgia Hudson talked to Lisa.

"I just wanted to tell you again that I'm sorry about what happened before," Jeff said. "With the branch."

"Well. Nobody got hurt."

"You looked pretty upset," he said. "I wanted to stick around and talk to you."

"I had to read, anyway."

"Right." Jeff paused. "How'd that go? Did you learn anything?"

Melanie hesitated. Why was he so interested. "Not really," she said. "It's kind of confusing."

"Well, you'll probably figure it out."

"Maybe."

"Melanie, are you okay?" he asked. "You sound kind of . . . I don't know. Like you've got a lot on your mind."

Oh, I do, Melanie thought. "I'm fine," she told him.

"Good." He paused again, then said, "I won't be seeing you out at the Randolphs' anymore."

"Why not? Oh, wait — did Ms. Hudson fire you?"

"Not exactly. She came out to the truck and asked me to tell her again what had happened," Jeff said. "So I did. She just listened and didn't say anything. Then when I got back to the landscaping office, the boss told me she'd called. She told him she wants somebody else to handle the Randolph grounds."

"Did she say why?"

"She told him she thought I was too young and inexperienced." Jeff laughed a little. "I guess she did me a favor. If she'd told him the real reason, I wouldn't be working for him anymore."

"So you're not fired from other yard jobs, just the Randolphs'."

"Which is good, probably. I won't have to see Garrett or Ms. Hudson," he said. "But I'll miss seeing Lisa. And you."

The thing to say was "we can see each other anytime." Melanie didn't say it.

"That's not the main reason I'm calling," Jeff went on. "I wondered if you wanted to see a movie tonight."

"No. I mean, I can't tonight," Melanie said. "I'm baby-sitting."

"Oh. Well. Okay." Jeff waited a moment. "How about tomorrow?"

"I'm not sure yet. Jeff, I have to go," Melanie said. "The dog's trying to dig under the fence out back."

Actually, Oliver was standing at the patio door, waiting to be let in. But Melanie couldn't keep listening to Jeff. She liked the sound of his voice. She liked his smile and the way he moved. She liked the feel of his lips on hers.

But she was afraid of him.

At eight that night, Melanie left lights blazing in every room of the house and walked two blocks down the street to her baby-sitting job at the Barretts'. She'd written out the rest of the lines Lisa had signaled on and she took the papers with her. The little girls' bedtime was eight-thirty. If she got lucky, they'd go to sleep fast and she could study all the quotes and try to make sense out of them.

At nine, Melanie tiptoed down the hall and

peeked into the bedroom. Both kids were asleep.

Back in the living room, Melanie settled on the couch and picked up the papers and read the quotes. Then she leaned back and thought about them.

*Somebody has plotted something*

*Eyes large and black*

*Something which used to make me fear and shrink*

*A gentleman in travelling clothes — a stranger*

*A group by the fire; a newcomer called Mason Help*

*An awful event*

*And dangerous he looked: his black eyes darted sparks*

*the pale, seemingly lifeless face of the stranger*

*A crime*

*Fire and blood in the darkest hours of the night*

*The commonplace stranger involved in a web of horror*

*The stranger who might be dying*

Melanie sat up suddenly.

The *stranger* was the one who was hurt, not the one with the dangerous dark eyes. So if Jeff was the stranger Lisa was talking about, maybe Melanie didn't have to be afraid of him.

She picked up the papers and read the list of quotes again.

In the book, the one with the dangerous dark eyes was Mr. Rochester. But Jane Eyre wasn't afraid of him. She loved him.

Melanie shook her head. She was confusing the actual story with the story Lisa was trying to tell her. Jeff could still be the dark-eyed stranger. He could still be dangerous. So could Georgia Hudson. Or Garrett, even though he wasn't a stranger to Lisa.

Tossing the papers down, Melanie went to the kitchen and got a soda. She was just sitting down on the couch again when the front door opened and Mrs. Barrett came in.

"Hi. You're really early," Melanie said.

Mrs. Barrett sighed. "Car trouble. John's on the highway, waiting for the AAA. He didn't want to leave it there, so he'll go to the garage with it and call a cab." She took off her coat and shook the raindrops off her hair. "I was lucky — some friends were behind us and gave me a ride home."

"Your night's kind of ruined, huh?"

Mrs. Barrett nodded, sighing again.

Melanie gathered her papers and stood up. "Well, everything's fine here," she said. "I guess I'll go on home."

Mrs. Barrett paid Melanie and thanked her

and gave her an umbrella. "It's starting to come down out there," she said.

Melanie said good night and stepped outside. The rain wasn't really that bad yet, but the fog was thick. Halfway down the front walk, she felt like she'd stepped into a wet, gray blanket.

She turned and looked back at the house. Even from such a short distance, the porch light looked fuzzy and dim. She opened the umbrella and started home.

The cars that drove by drove slowly, their headlights almost swallowed by the fog. Most houses had a porch light on, but they looked as small as penlights and reached about as far.

It was cold and wet and eerie. The fog swirled around like damp, slithery scarves.

Melanie remembered the dream she'd had of driving up the road to the Randolph house and seeing Jeff Singer standing there.

Jeff. Smiling as he urged her off the edge of the cliff.

She shivered and walked faster.

At the end of the first block, she stopped to look for cars. The roads were slick. Even if a driver's headlights could pick her out, it might be too late. She could get hit and die out here.

Stop thinking of dying, she told herself.

One car crept past. Melanie couldn't even tell what color it was. The whole world was gray. She stepped off the curb and hurried across the street.

One more block to go. One more street to cross and she'd be home.

The rain was coming harder now. Melanie was glad of the umbrella, but she wished she'd asked for a flashlight. It might help her see a few inches ahead, at least. Now, all there was, was fog . . . thick fog.

When she reached the end of the second block, her sneaker slid on the wet curb and she stumbled into the street. The umbrella shot out of her hands and she fell to her knees, hitting the one she'd skinned earlier.

She found the umbrella, picked herself up, and started across the street. Her house was the second from the corner.

When she was in front of the first house, she could make out the misty glow of the carriage light at the end of her driveway. Her knee hurt but she picked up her pace.

Just as she started to cross her driveway, the lights hit her.

Bright lights. Aimed right at her. Melanie squinted. All she saw was fog, swirling around two yellow lights.

What was it? What was back there?

Then Melanie heard a sound. A low, rumbling noise.

And then she knew what was behind the lights. It was a car. A car with fog lights, sitting far back in her driveway.

Suddenly, the engine rumbled. The car shot forward, its lights piercing the fog.

Melanie stood frozen in their glare like a deer on a highway.

# Chapter 14

The low-slung fog lights glowed brighter as the car accelerated down the driveway toward the street.

Straight toward Melanie.

Run! she told herself.

But she couldn't move. She stood transfixed, clutching the umbrella.

The car engine roared. The lights loomed closer.

A voice inside Melanie's head screamed at her to run.

Inside the house, Oliver barked hoarsely. Finally, Melanie's blood started flowing again. Her legs unlocked and now she could move.

With a scream that shattered the quiet of the street, she dived out of the way of the oncoming car and landed stomach-down in the soggy grass of her front yard.

The car's tires spun and whined on the wet

pavement. Scrambling to her knees, Melanie looked back just in time to see its taillights moving down the street. They flared like matches for a moment, and then the fog snuffed them out.

The car was gone.

Melanie sat back on her heels, her heart racing. The dog was still barking, frantic now from hearing her scream.

Then Melanie heard a voice from across the street. "What's going on over there?" It was Trina's voice. "Hey!" she called sharply. "Who's out here?"

"It's me." Melanie's voice was quavery and not very loud. She took a shaky breath. "It's me. Melanie!" she called out.

She heard footsteps on the street, and then Trina appeared like a ghost out of the fog. "Mel, are you okay?" she asked. She took Melanie's arm and pulled her to her feet. "What happened? I was putting some mail out for tomorrow morning, and I heard this blood-curdling scream. I thought somebody was getting killed!"

"So did I." Melanie's teeth were chattering. "That's why I screamed. I thought I was going to die."

"Geez, you're not kidding, are you?" Trina said.

Melanie shook her head. Her hands were muddy and plastered with blades of grass. Her knee hurt. But she was alive.

For now.

She looked toward the street. "That car," she said. "It wasn't somebody just turning around in the driveway. It was facing the street. I was standing right there in the lights and it didn't slow down. It went faster. It was so awful!"

"Wait a sec," Trina said. "Are you saying what I think you're saying? That it tried to run you down?"

Melanie nodded, thinking. Garrett's car wasn't that big and neither was Jeff's. Jeff's truck was, but it didn't have fog lights. None of them did. She had no idea what Ms. Hudson drove.

But *someone* had tried to kill her.

"Melanie?" Trina said. Her blond hair was frizzy from the damp and she looked scared. "What's going on?"

Melanie said in a choking voice, "Come on, let's go inside."

Melanie unlocked the door and they went in. The dog quieted down, then started sniffing her knees.

Melanie leaned against the wall, but she didn't move any farther into the house. "I don't want to go in," she said. "I know Oliver would be barking if somebody was here. But I'm afraid I'll find another message. Help me look around, okay?"

There were no messages. No bloodred writing on the doors or mirrors, no notes, no ugly voice on the answering machine.

Upstairs, Melanie took off her wet clothes. Her hands shook as she put a Band-Aid on her knee. She wrapped herself in a long white bathrobe and put thick socks on her feet. But she couldn't get warm.

She couldn't stop shivering.

Somebody had tried to *kill* her.

Down in the kitchen, Trina handed Melanie a mug of tea. "You look like hell," she said bluntly. "Would you mind telling me what's going on now?"

"I told you before," Melanie said, warming her hands on the mug. "Somebody doesn't want me finding out Lisa's secret."

Trina's mouth fell open. "And you think they just tried to run you down? Mel, are you serious?"

"Whoever was driving that car was serious!" Melanie shouted. "Does it sound like just a coincidence to you, after everything else that's happened?"

"No, I guess not. But, Melanie, who?" Trina asked. "Who'd do such . . . crazy things?"

"Crazy? Then how about Garrett?" Melanie said. "Or Georgia Hudson? She's crazy about Lisa's dad, I can tell. Maybe she wants Lisa out of the way." She paused. "Or maybe it's Jeff."

"Jeff?" Trina's eyes widened. "Do you really believe that?"

"I'm afraid not to," Melanie said.

"But wait." Trina thought a second. "Jeff couldn't have put that note in the book, could he? Wouldn't somebody have seen him on a monitor?"

"Maybe not." Melanie pulled the blind away from the patio doors and peered out. All she saw was fog. "It wouldn't take very long. Ms. Hudson doesn't watch the monitor every second."

"He's not the only one who could have done it, though," Trina said.

"Right." Melanie dropped the blind against the glass and started pacing. Her heart wouldn't slow down. She couldn't keep still. "If I just knew what Lisa's trying to say, then I'd know who's after me."

Trina got herself a soda. "Go over those places where Lisa signaled you," she said, popping the tab on the can. "Maybe something'll hit me."

Melanie got the papers — wrinkled from being in her shorts' pocket — and smoothed them out on the kitchen table. She finished the tea and paced some more while Trina read them.

When Trina finished reading, the two of them talked about the quotes and came up with about ten different stories Lisa could be trying to tell.

"We're just making things up," Melanie said finally. "The only one who really knows is Lisa."

Trina nodded. "Hey, I've got an idea," she said. "Why don't you write a bunch of questions and *show* them to her? Nobody would be able to read them on a monitor."

"No, but they'd be able to tell what I was doing."

"So hide them in a magazine," Trina said. "Pretend you found some fascinating article or you're showing her pictures or something."

It wasn't a bad idea, Melanie thought. And it was much better than what she'd been doing — trying to figure out everything on her own. She should have thought of it two days ago.

Trina decided to spend the night. After she called home, she and Melanie spent a little while longer talking about what questions to ask and how to phrase them.

Melanie's parents called to see if she was okay. With tears running down her cheeks, she said she was.

*So far,* Melanie thought later when she got into bed. So far she was still alive.

But how long would it last?

Trina had already left for work when Melanie woke the next morning. Still nervous from the night before, she locked the bathroom door when she took a shower, and didn't let Oliver stay outside long. The fog had thinned, but it wasn't completely gone. A fine rain came down steadily.

At the kitchen table, she cut up strips of paper and taped them on pages of an entertainment magazine. Then she started printing questions on them for Lisa to read.

The first question was the key: Was there a crime?

Melanie was almost sure of the answer. Anyone desperate enough to try to kill her had to be hiding a crime.

Suddenly, only the first question mattered. If Lisa *did* blink yes to it, then Melanie would call the police.

It was eleven o'clock. Over two hours before she was supposed to be at the Randolphs'.

But Melanie couldn't wait. Pulling a sweat-shirt on over her T-shirt and jeans, she grabbed the magazine and left the house.

Fear was making her heart race again. But the fear wasn't just for herself. It was for Lisa, too. She was in danger, too.

Lisa was a much easier target than Melanie. Melanie could run if she had to. She could fight. She could scream.

But Lisa couldn't walk or even speak. Lisa was trapped.

# Chapter 15

The policeman's yellow slicker glistened with rain and dripped water onto Melanie's sleeve as he leaned into her open car window.

"Can't go up there, miss," he said.

Melanie was at the foot of the cliff road, behind two barriers with blinking orange lights on them. "Why not?" Melanie said. "What's the matter?" Nerves made her voice shrill.

"Nothing to get excited about," he said, looking at her strangely. "Mud slide. A couple of trees down about halfway up. You just can't drive up yet, that's all."

Melanie relaxed slightly. Visions of Lisa being stalked and hurt faded for a moment. But then she *had* to get to her. She couldn't wait.

"Listen, I have to get to the house at the top," she said.

"The Randolphs'?"

Melanie nodded. "I have a job there. Isn't there another way up?"

The policeman straightened up and rivulets of water rolled down his slicker. He looked around, then leaned on Melanie's door again. "Well, you can drive around on Route Nine, back of the woods," he said. "There's an old dirt road that cuts off into the trees. I know it heads up toward the Randolph house, but how far it goes . . . ?" He shrugged and shook his head, pelting Melanie's sleeve with more raindrops. "You'd be better off calling, saying you'll be late."

"You're probably right," Melanie said. "Thanks."

He straightened up again and touched the brim of his plastic-covered hat. Melanie smiled.

Then she backed the car up and drove off toward Route 9.

She had to get to Lisa.

The flat part of the cliff road merged into Route 9, so Melanie didn't have any trouble finding her way. It took her in a broad curve, then straightened out after about five minutes. On her right, she could see the thick forest stretching up gradually toward the cliff. She couldn't see the Randolph house; it was probably a mile or more away.

It wasn't long before she saw the turnoff. Just as he'd said, it cut off toward the right; into the woods. And it was dirt. Mud, actually. But once she drove a few yards, the mud wasn't too bad. The trees were so thick their branches made a canopy overhead. It hadn't kept the road dry, but she was pretty sure she wouldn't get stuck.

Wet branches slapped against the car windows as Melanie drove farther into the woods. It was dark under the trees. She turned her high beams on.

The road sloped gradually uphill, but not in a straight line. It meandered through the trees. Melanie tried to judge whether she was to the right or the left of the Randolph house. Maybe she'd get lucky and it would come out right at the back, where the lawn met the forest.

She hadn't gone very far — maybe only half a mile — when she took her foot off the gas to let the car ease itself through a deep rut.

The car rumbled, started to shake, and died.

It started up again immediately. Melanie let it idle a minute. Then she put her foot on the brake to shift into drive. The car shook and died again.

Melanie started the car again. And again.

But every time she took her foot off the gas, the engine shuddered to a stop.

Melanie turned off the headlights and sat for a minute, listening to water splattering on the roof.

Okay. Route 9 wasn't very far behind her. She could walk back to it. Then what? Hitchhike? Not a great idea. She might be able to flag down a police car or a tow truck. But if she didn't see one, she'd have to walk all the way back to town.

Or she could keep walking up this road, toward the Randolph house. She knew she wouldn't get lost, and it wasn't that far.

She *had* to get there.

Melanie got out and slid the rolled-up magazine into a back pocket of her jeans, pulling her sweatshirt over it so it wouldn't get wet. She locked the car, put the keys in her pocket, and started walking.

As the forest closed in on her, Melanie shivered. It was like moving through a dark, damp cave. Fog drifted through the trees like something alive. Water dripped onto her head and rolled down her neck. She felt cold all over.

Keep going, she told herself.

A sudden noise made her jump. It sounded like a twig snapping. Had somebody followed her?

Her heart thudding in her ears, Melanie tried to listen. There it was again. A snapping, rustling sound. And then a shrill cry overhead.

Just a bird.

Get a grip, she told herself. Nobody's out here but you.

She kept going. Low-growing ferns whipped at her jeans and her sneakers gradually turned brown with mud. The magazine poked her in the back.

She was shifting it to her other pocket when she suddenly realized that the road had come to an end.

It wasn't a gradual end. Suddenly, there was simply no more road, just forest.

For a moment, Melanie was tempted to turn around and walk back. But then she saw a slight opening through the mass of trees.

A footpath? Somebody must have walked through these woods sometime. Maybe even Lisa. After all, this was her property.

It *was* a path. It was overrun with trailing vines and once in awhile a fallen tree, so it hadn't been walked on much lately. But it was definitely a path.

Melanie took it.

It was much harder going. Vines snagged her jeans and branches grabbed at her hair. And the forest was starting to smell. No wonder, Melanie thought. Nothing ever got much chance to dry out around here. Things rotted from the damp in the thick woods.

She breathed through her mouth and kept going.

After about twenty minutes of very slow walking, the path opened up on a small clearing. There were a few fallen trees around the edge of it, and Melanie sat down on one. She had to rest, just for a minute or two.

Still breathing through her mouth because of the smell, Melanie looked around and saw a bunch of rocks in the middle of the clearing. Some were scattered, but the rest were still in a ragged half-circle.

A campfire.

Suddenly, Melanie remembered: Heather told her that Lisa had invited the backpacker to camp on her property. What had she said? *The woods go on for miles behind the house and the Randolphs own it all.*

Getting up, Melanie went over and stared down at the fire-blackened rocks.

This could be where he'd camped. Peter Something. North or Norton. A great-looking guy with dark hair and a silver snake on top of his black walking stick.

He'd camped here and then left.

And it was around the same time Lisa fell.

Could he be the one Lisa was trying to tell her about?

But if he'd gone, then who was after Melanie?

She didn't know. Only Lisa knew. Time to get going.

She took a deep breath through her nose and winced. The smell was worse. A sickly, sweet smell, like rotting garbage. She couldn't wait to get out of these woods.

The path was even less of a path now. The roots and vines were so thick in places that Melanie wasn't even sure she was following a trail at all. Some of the vines had thorns. When she wiped her forehead, her hand came away bloody.

Melanie had to walk slowly, stepping high to avoid the vines and roots. But it was impossible to avoid them all. She took a step, felt a vine twist tight around her ankle, and started to fall. Unable to catch her balance, she went sprawling face down in wet leaves and pine needles and soft, slithery muck.

As Melanie dragged her hands back to boost herself up, her fingers caught on something. She thought it was a vine, but she was wrong.

It was some kind of woven strap.

Melanie dropped it and sat back on her knees. Sat back on something hard and knobby. A rock, probably. Pain shot through her knee and she got to her feet. Some of the muck came with her, clinging to her sweatshirt and the front of her jeans.

She started to wipe it off.

And stopped, staring at the ground in front of her.

It was the hard, knobby thing she'd felt under her knee.

But it wasn't a rock.

Slowly, Melanie bent over, grabbed hold, and pulled.

When she straightened up again, she was holding a black walking stick with a coiled silver snake on the top.

# Chapter 16

The snake's wedge-shaped head rested on its top coil.

One of its eyes had a tiny chip of red glass in it. The other eye was empty.

The empty eye stared up at Melanie.

The backpacker *had* been here, she thought.

But when he left, he didn't take his walking stick with him.

Why not?

Bending over again, Melanie tugged on the strap she'd grabbed hold of when she fell. Matted leaves and mud shifted. She yanked, and the strap came free in her hand. There was some material clinging to it. Nylon. The kind of stuff backpacks were made from.

He hadn't taken his backpack, either.

Why?

He'd camped here, the weekend Lisa fell.

Maybe he'd never left. Maybe he'd done something that Lisa knew about.

*What crime was this?*

He could have done something terrible. And then he'd left his things here. Buried them, so everyone would think he'd gone.

He might be hanging around *somewhere*, to make sure Lisa didn't tell.

But he couldn't know she was trying to tell. Unless he'd found some way to watch.

Nervously, Melanie tightened her grip on the walking stick and looked around. She thought she was alone in the woods.

Maybe she wasn't.

She had to keep going.

She took the stick with her. She might need it.

The woods seemed darker than ever. Melanie wished that she'd taken the policeman's advice and called the Randolph house. Or at least walked back to Route 9 when her car died.

The smell was better, though. Only a few minutes away from the clearing, she hardly noticed it. She could smell damp leaves but the other smell was almost gone.

The other smell. The sweet, sickly smell of something rotting.

Melanie stopped walking.

She remembered some lines from the book, lines that Lisa had tapped on: *"This commonplace, quiet stranger — how had he become involved in the web of horror? He moaned so, and looked so weak, wild and lost, I feared he was dying."*

Melanie looked back in the direction of the clearing. There'd been a campfire there.

*"I was now able to concentrate my attention on the group by the fire, and I presently gathered that the newcomer was called Mr. Mason."*

In *Jane Eyre*, the stranger named Mason got hurt. He looked as if he were dying, but he lived.

But what if the stranger named Peter hadn't lived?

Melanie was sure Peter had buried his walking stick and backpack on purpose. She'd been sure he was hanging around, scaring Lisa. What if she was wrong?

What if Peter had been buried, too?

Melanie looked down at the walking stick. There was a roaring in her ears like wind. She felt dizzy, sick.

The stick belongs to a dead man, she thought. A man who was buried somewhere near it, along with his backpack.

Melanie had fallen on his grave.

She had to get out of here. Had to get to Lisa!

With a cry, she plunged into the trees, jumping over vines and using the walking stick to bat away low-hanging branches.

It doesn't have to be true, she tried to tell herself. The backpacker didn't *have* to be dead.

But then she remembered the smell, and she ran faster.

The vines snagged her clothes and tore her skin. Melanie tried to step around them, or trample them down, but they were everywhere. Her side started to ache and she gasped for breath.

Finally, she had to stop, just for a few seconds. Leaning on the stick, she closed her eyes.

When her breath was nearly back to normal, she raised her head and looked around.

And saw something shiny hanging from a narrow branch only a foot away from her eyes.

It was a thin gold chain with a gold heart on it. A necklace. Lisa's necklace, the one Garrett looked for but couldn't find. The one he thought Jeff took.

But Jeff didn't take it. And Garrett couldn't find it where Lisa fell because that wasn't where it came off. It came off here, in the woods. A tree branch snagged it and ripped it off, leaving an ugly red mark around Lisa's neck.

Melanie reached out and pulled the necklace from the branch. The chain was broken. It must have hurt when the branch caught it and pulled it tight against her neck. Why hadn't Lisa stopped?

She must have been running. Like Melanie. Running from something.

Or somebody.

Melanie shoved the necklace in her pocket and took off again. Questions tumbled through her mind, but she didn't try to answer them. Only Lisa could answer them. She had to get to Lisa.

After a little while, Melanie realized she wasn't swinging the walking stick at branches so much. And she wasn't stopping so often to untangle vines from around her ankles. The path had cleared up a bit.

She was getting close.

She took one running step and tripped on a root. The walking stick shot out of her hand and went flying ahead of her. Catching her balance, she went to pick it up, but she couldn't see it. She pushed through some branches.

And stepped into a void.

With a scream, she reached out, just managing to wrap one arm around a tree trunk.

Slowly, carefully, she eased her feet onto solid ground.

She was standing right at the edge of the cliff. A deep gash in the earth about fifteen feet wide. And much, much deeper. Tree limbs and rocks had tumbled down the sides into the bottom. That's where the walking stick had fallen.

If she had fallen with it, she might be dead. Or paralyzed, like Lisa . . .

With a shudder, Melanie took another step back and looked across the deep ravine. Through the fine mist, she saw a dim light, and the hazy outlines of a house.

The Randolph house. She was standing right across from it, where the cliff edge cut back into the woods. She'd finally made it.

Lisa never had. She'd been running back to her house that night. Running in terror. Her necklace caught on a branch, but she didn't stop to take it off. She kept running. But it was dark, and she didn't see the cliff edge until it was too late.

Lisa hadn't been as lucky as Melanie.

Carefully, Melanie crept close to the cliff again. There was no way she could cross here. She looked back and forth, wondering whether to go toward the front of the house or the back. The back, she decided. There was just more cliff at the front.

It took a few minutes, but finally the gap narrowed and became a shallow ditch. Melanie jumped across it, then headed for the house.

When she stepped out of the woods, she was at the far end of the yard. Straight ahead, she could see the terrace and the French doors at the back of the library.

She looked toward the garages. No cars were parked outside. Good. Lisa didn't have any visitors. Melanie only had Georgia Hudson to worry about.

When she was halfway up the walk, the back door opened.

Garrett was standing there.

Georgia Hudson, Garrett, or Jeff, Melanie thought. Until she talked to Lisa, she couldn't trust any of them.

"Mel," Garrett said. He pushed his sunglasses up on his head and peered at her. "What happened to you?"

Melanie looked down. Her jeans and sweatshirt were covered with mud and gunk. Her hands were crisscrossed with scratches. Her fingernails were black.

"I . . . there was a mud slide," she said. Her throat felt raw. "The police told me a tree was down and I couldn't drive up. So I walked."

Garrett said with surprise, "You look like you crawled."

Melanie looked down at her clothes. "I fell."

"You okay? You've got blood on your face."

Melanie stared past him. "Where's Ms. Hudson?"

"She went to pick up Mr. Randolph at the airport," Garrett said. "She left before the road was closed, but she called a little while ago and said the plane's delayed because of the fog."

"So you're staying with Lisa?" Melanie asked. "I didn't see your car. Did you walk up, too?"

Garrett shook his head and his sunglasses slipped back down. "I got here before the slide and put the car in one of the garages," he said. "It's got a problem in the rain. When some of the wires get wet, it won't start. I'm hoping it'll dry off in the garage."

"Speaking of getting wet," Melanie said. "Can I come in?"

Garrett stepped aside. "Sorry about that."

"I was just telling Lisa you probably wouldn't make it because of the road," Garrett said. "I thought you'd call."

"I probably should have," Melanie said.

"Listen, point me to a bathroom, will you? I've got to wash up."

There was a bathroom across the hall from the library. Melanie quickly washed her hands and face, wincing as the soap stung the scratches. Garrett was right, she thought, glancing into the mirror. She looked like she'd crawled up here. Right now she had to talk to Lisa.

She gulped down some water, then hurried into the library.

Lisa was facing the windows. Garrett was sitting in front of her on the same ottoman Melanie used.

Was he going to stay here the whole time? Melanie wondered. She wanted him out. She didn't trust him. She didn't trust anybody but Lisa.

"Ah, the reader!" Garrett said, standing up. "I think Lisa's glad you're here, Melanie. Probably bored with me by now."

Melanie crossed the room. "Hi, Lisa."

"Mel had some problems getting here," Garrett explained to Lisa. "I was telling you about the road, remember? You won't believe what she did — she hiked up here."

"I didn't want to disappoint you," Melanie said.

Lisa stared back, her eyes wide. Then her glance shifted to Garrett.

"Oh, right," Garrett said. "It's reading time. Don't mind me." He walked over to the couch near the side windows and stretched out on his back. "Couldn't do this if Hawkeye Hudson was here," he said with a grin.

Melanie had to get rid of him. She couldn't talk to Lisa with Garrett in the room. "Are you going to stay here while I read?" she asked.

"Sure," Garrett said. "I won't interrupt."

"Maybe not, but . . . it'll make me nervous."

"Really?"

"Yes." Melanie made herself smile. "It will."

Garrett uncrossed his legs.

Good, Melanie thought. He was going to leave. She looked at Lisa again. And felt her mouth go dry.

Lisa's finger was tapping on the chair arm. Tapping frantically.

Lisa was terrified.

Melanie looked back to the couch.

Garrett was just sitting up. As he moved, the lamp next to the couch reflected off the lens of his sunglasses. The flash of light only lasted a second. But that was long enough.

As Melanie stared at the big, black sunglasses, the words from *Jane Eyre* flew into her mind.

*"And dangerous he looked: his black eyes darted sparks."*

Garrett, Melanie thought.

Garrett is the dark-eyed stranger.

# Chapter 17

Melanie's heart slammed against her chest so hard she was dizzy.

A trap. She'd walked right into a trap!

The blood thundered in her ears. She had to get out. Get help.

Without meaning to, she took a step backward.

No. Don't move. Don't show you know.

A phone, she thought. Talk your way out of this room and get to a phone.

Garrett was on his feet now, looking at her. *Eyes large and black.* Why hadn't she seen it?

Melanie swallowed and tried to keep her face from showing anything. He might leave, she thought. Ms. Hudson and Mr. Randolph would be coming back. He might give up for now and leave.

If he doesn't, get out of here and find a phone.

Garrett slid the glasses up to the top of his head. His eyes were blue now, but just as dangerous-looking. "You look a little nervous, Mel," he said.

She didn't try to smile. She couldn't fake it. "I told you," she said. "I can't read with anybody else in here." Her voice surprised her. She thought it would be shaking. Her stomach was, and her hands. But her voice sounded normal. "I think I'll wait until you leave."

"That might be awhile. Mud slide, remember?"

"Well, I could hike back down the road and see if it's clear."

"Don't bother, Melanie."

"It's not a bother. I — "

"No, you don't get it," Garrett interrupted. "I mean don't bother trying to hide what you feel. You're not any good at it." His voice was flat. No emotion at all. "It's obvious that you know."

Melanie glanced at the windows. Not even the cat was around.

"You're not thinking of going, are you?" Garrett said. "Leaving Lisa? That wouldn't be very nice."

Melanie looked at Lisa. "I'm not leaving."

"Well, that's good," Garrett said. "I mean, you two have some kind of special communication going, am I right? Wouldn't want to break that up."

Melanie didn't say anything.

"Am I right?" Garrett said again. "You and Lisa have been telling each other secrets? No, wait. That's wrong." He smiled. "Lisa's been telling *you* a secret. That's the way it's been going."

"You already know she has," Melanie said.

He nodded. "You figured out what it is yet?"

"Not all of it."

"No?" Garrett raised an eyebrow. "Well, you're not as smart as I thought, Mel. But you sure are stubborn. You wouldn't stop, would you? You'd have kept at it until you got it all."

"I've figured out a little." Melanie reached into her pocket and pulled out Lisa's broken necklace. "I know where Lisa lost this."

When Lisa saw the necklace, she sucked in her breath and made a high-pitched humming sound. Melanie dropped the broken chain and kicked it across the floor. It skittered to a stop at Garrett's feet.

"I found Peter's walking stick, too," Melanie went on. "And part of his backpack."

Lisa's humming broke off. Melanie looked

at her. "I know you saw something horrible," she said. "I remember the line from the book — *"what awful event has taken place?"* Whatever you saw made you run. Maybe the woods were foggy that night, too. Maybe the fog looked like smoke and that's why you tapped on the part about wandering through volcanic-looking hills."

Lisa blinked.

"Your necklace caught on a tree branch, but you didn't stop," Melanie said. "You were terrified. You wanted to get home. But it was dark and you couldn't tell exactly where you were going. And when you came to the edge of the cliff out there, you were running too fast to catch yourself."

Lisa closed her eyes and kept them closed for a moment. Then she dragged them open. It was a slow, sad, yes.

"I don't know exactly what you saw," Melanie said. "I think I know part of it, but not all. And I don't know why." She looked at Garrett. "Why don't *you* tell me?"

Keep talking, she thought. Maybe Georgia Hudson and Mr. Randolph would come back in time.

"Sure, why not?" Garrett said. "It'll be our secret, right?" He bent down and picked up the broken necklace. "Let's see, where to start? Well, you obviously know about Peter. Peter the Great. After Neil punched him, we thought he'd leave. But no, Lisa invited him to set up camp, right on her property."

Melanie swallowed dryly. She glanced at the camera. Nobody was watching. Nobody knew what was happening.

"Neil and I knew where he was camping, so we decided to pay him a visit," Garrett went on. He smiled again. "Kind of urge him to pack up and get going, you know? We drove part of the way in on that old road off Route Nine and walked the rest of the way. He had a little fire going when we got there. Nice and cozy. So we joined him."

The group by the fire, Melanie thought. Lisa had seen them.

"And we made our suggestion: that he leave," Garrett said. "He pretty much told us to get lost. Said Lisa had to be the one to tell him to go, since she was the one who'd invited him to stay." He glanced at Lisa. His eyes were as cold and as flat as his voice. "Neil was already mad because of what happened the day before. What Peter said just made him madder, so he jumped him. But Peter was strong, and a much better fighter than Neil. So I had to help out. Not that I minded. I was pretty mad, too."

Melanie cleared her throat. "I don't get it. What were you so mad about?"

"Because *she* wanted to break up with me," Garrett said, pointing at Lisa.

Lisa's eyes were locked on Melanie's. She blinked.

"That's why I was mad," Garrett went on. "Oh, the breaking up didn't have anything to do with Peter the Great. She told me about that before he showed up at the diner. But anyway, I was in a pretty lousy state of mind, and Peter — well, he was just in the wrong place at the wrong time."

*"This commonplace, quiet stranger,"* Melanie thought. Now she knew how he'd become involved in the "web of horror."

"So. It was the two of us against the backpacker. We won," Garrett said. "He was on his knees, and Neil and I decided to take off. Neil was way ahead of me. I was almost out of the clearing when Peter jumped on my back."

While Garrett talked, he twisted the thin gold chain around his fingers. "When I went down, I felt something under my hand. I didn't even think. Just grabbed hold of it and turned around and swung it at his head as hard as I could."

And killed him, Melanie thought.

"It was a rock. It killed him." Garrett looked at Lisa again. Finally, there was something in his eyes. Pain. And anger. "It was an accident, Lisa! And I didn't know you saw it. What were you doing there, anyway?"

Lisa stayed still.

Melanie wondered what she was doing there, too. Bringing food to Peter? Maybe she was attracted to him, like everybody else, and just wanted an excuse to see him.

"I left him there," Garrett said. "Caught up to Neil. I didn't tell him what happened. He still doesn't know. I drove him home and came back and buried Peter."

Melanie closed her eyes. The mystery in fire and blood. Lisa had seen it.

"I didn't know you were there," Garrett said to Lisa again. "But then Melanie started talking about some message you were trying to give her. And I started to wonder. You never moved or anything when I was with you. Your eyes never looked happy to see me. I knew you wanted to break up, but I still thought you'd be glad when I came to visit. But you weren't. You didn't look at me much, and when you did, you looked . . . scared. And mad sometimes."

She looks the same way now, Melanie thought. Scared. But angry, too.

"So after Melanie told me about your 'message,' I started to wonder," Garrett said. "I wasn't sure, but I tried to scare her off, just in case. Then I heard some of the stuff she was reading to you, and I *was* sure. God, I didn't know what to do. I just knew I couldn't let her find out."

But I did, Melanie thought. She wished she hadn't, but it was too late.

Garrett walked across the room and stood in front of Lisa. "It was an accident, Lisa!" he said again. "I didn't mean to kill him, you've got to know that. Why did you have to tell?"

Lisa stared at him. There were tears in her eyes, but she blinked them back. Then she looked away from his face.

Garrett looked at her for a moment longer, then walked away. He slid the broken necklace into his jeans pocket and pulled the dark glasses back down over his eyes.

Melanie's heartbeat speeded up.

"Story time's over," Garrett said calmly. "Everybody knows everything. Our secret, right?" He laughed softly. "Wrong. I know you couldn't keep it to yourself, Mel. And even if you promised to, well . . . Lisa would find some other way to tell."

Why wasn't Georgia Hudson back yet? Melanie wondered frantically. The fog wasn't so bad anymore. The plane must have landed. The road had to be clear. Where *was* she?

"Time to get going," Garrett said suddenly.

He reached into his back pocket and pulled out a knife.

Oh, God! He'll use it, Melanie thought, her heart racing faster. He's desperate. He tried to kill you once. Nothing's going to stop him this time!

"Don't look like that, Melanie," he said. "It's not what you think." He turned the knife over in his hands. "This is just to persuade you to come for a walk."

The roaring in Melanie's ears was so loud she could hardly hear him. Her knees felt like jelly. Somehow, she made her way across the room to Lisa.

"Good," Garrett said. "That's just what I had in mind. Lisa doesn't get outside enough, right? So you're going to take her for a little walk."

Melanie put her hand on Lisa's shoulder. She swallowed hard. "For a walk?" she said, gesturing toward the windows and the mist outside. "Nobody would believe I'd take her out in this."

"But that's what they'll have to believe," Garrett told her. "See, I'll say when you showed up to read, I went out to the garage to try to get my car started. I never expected you to do something so dumb as taking her outside, I'll say. So I was busy with the car for awhile, and when I came back and saw you were gone, I couldn't believe it."

Melanie tightened her hand on Lisa's shoulder. "And then what?"

"Then I tried to find you, what else?" Garrett waved his hand toward the windows on the far side of the library. "One of those windows was open, and when I looked out, I saw . . . well, come see for yourself."

Garrett waved the knife, motioning for Melanie to come over.

Melanie waited a second, then slowly crossed the room.

"Look out the windows," Garrett said from behind her. "Go on."

Melanie walked closer to the windows and looked out. Two narrow steps led down to the side yard. A wide plank was leaning against them.

A ramp for a wheelchair.

"See the plank?" Garrett asked. "That's what I'll tell them I saw, too. Open window, plank . . . you had to be out there somewhere, right?"

Melanie turned around and stared at him.

"So, naturally, I went out to look," Garrett said. "I was really worried. I yelled real loud, but you didn't answer. I kept yelling and walking up and down, trying to find you. Finally, I did."

Garrett lifted his glasses and looked at Melanie. His cold, empty eyes made her shiver.

"You're wondering where I found you, aren't you, Mel?"

Don't think about it, Melanie told herself. If you think about where he's going to "find" you, then he'll win. Think about beating him.

"Well, it's time to find out," Garrett said. "Come on, Melanie, let's go outside."

Melanie took a slow, deep breath and went back to Lisa.

"Come on, Mel." Garrett's voice had an edge to it now. Sharp, like the knife.

Melanie went behind Lisa's chair and took hold of the handles.

"Okay. Let's go." Garrett waved the knife.

She could shove it into him, Melanie was thinking. Shove the chair real hard. Maybe push him down.

But he'd realize what she was doing. He'd just jump out of the way. And what about Lisa? Melanie could run, but Lisa would be trapped.

Think! She had to think of something else. And she had to do it fast.

"Last chance, Mel. Let's get going." Garrett pulled his glasses over his eyes.

And Melanie felt her blood run cold.

# Chapter 18

The room spun sickeningly. Everything looked fuzzy and far away.

If she blacked out, it would all be over.

Melanie reached out to steady herself. Her hand touched Lisa's shoulder again.

Slowly, the room stopped turning. Things came into focus again. Melanie took hold of the chair handles and pushed.

"Faster than that," Garrett said impatiently. "She's not heavy."

Melanie ignored him. She didn't hurry. But it didn't take long to push Lisa across the room.

Still facing them, Garrett reached behind him and unlatched one of the tall doors. Then he walked around until he was standing behind Melanie.

She couldn't see the knife anymore, but she knew it was pointed at her. The muscles in her back were rigid.

"Go on," Garrett said quietly.

Melanie pushed the chair out the window and over the lip of the plank, bracing her legs as the chair tilted down toward the lawn. Careful, she thought. If you let go, the chair will roll straight down and over the cliff.

*The cliff.*

Terror slammed through Melanie's heart again.

She knew what Garrett was going to do. He was going to force them *both* over the cliff. It would be another accident.

But this time, it would be deadly.

Her nerves hummed like power lines. Her hands were slick with sweat. Time was running out.

When the wheelchair was down the ramp, Garrett leaped down lightly beside Melanie. They were on a flagstone walk leading toward the front of the house. He pointed the knife in that direction.

Melanie felt a tiny bit of relief. She had thought it would happen right here. Now she had some time. Not much, but a little. *Use it!* she told herself. Use it to think of a way out!

"Go on," Garrett said, pointing with the knife again. "We'll take a stroll up there, away from these windows. Maybe they'll think you took her up front to welcome Dad home. And the edge was slippery and . . . well, you get the idea."

The flagstone walk was slick from the rain and mist and the wheels slipped a little when Melanie turned the chair. The walk sloped up, she noticed. The incline got steeper and steeper.

Melanie pushed, pretending it was harder than it was.

One chance. She had one chance. It had to work.

She couldn't do it alone, though. She'd need Lisa. And there was no way she could explain. But Lisa's mind worked just fine. She'd understand. She had to.

Melanie glanced over her shoulder. Garrett was about ten feet behind her.

She pushed the chair, until the walk was at its steepest. She glanced back again. Garrett was the same distance behind her. He might hear her voice, but he wouldn't know what she said.

Now!

Pretending to trip, Melanie lurched forward over the back of the wheelchair. Quickly, covering her movement with her body, she yanked the brake lever up. Then she took Lisa's hand and put it on the lever.

"Can you release it?" she whispered. Lisa blinked once. "Do it when I say his name."

"What's going on?" Garrett called out.

Melanie straightened up and turned around. He'd stopped walking.

"She's terrified," Melanie said. "I was trying to tell her everything will be all right. I don't think she believes me."

Garrett waved the knife. "Keep going."

Melanie gripped the chair handles again and pushed. The chair lurched, and she struggled with it, turning it sideways. "It's stuck," she called out.

Garrett stayed where he was. "Unstick it, Mel!"

Melanie shoved at the chair again and managed to turn it so it was facing Garrett. She stepped in front of it. "It's not working. It won't go."

"Fix it, Melanie! Get it going!"

Melanie took a deep breath and started walking downhill, toward Garrett.

He held the knife out. "Don't do that, Melanie. Get back up there with Lisa."

Melanie walked a little faster. Garrett watched her, but he didn't move.

When Melanie got just a few feet from him,

she stepped off the walk onto the wet grass. She veered toward the house until she was past him, then moved back onto the sidewalk and stopped.

Melanie was downhill from Garrett now. Lisa was at the top. Garrett was in the middle. He pivoted around, keeping his eyes on Melanie. His back was to Lisa.

He was right where Melanie wanted him.

"I'm not going to do it, Garrett!" she shouted. "I'm not going to help you stage an accident. You'll have to do it yourself, Garrett!"

Don't look back, Garrett, she thought. Don't look behind you.

"I know what you've got in mind for us, Garrett," she shouted. "If you think I'm going to help you, you're crazy!"

Melanie didn't dare shift her eyes. Garrett might turn around and see what was happening.

Lisa had done it. She'd released the brake and now the wheelchair was rolling down the walk. Straight toward Garrett.

The chair was gathering speed now. It wasn't silent, but Melanie kept her voice loud and prayed Garrett wouldn't hear it. "I can't believe what you're trying to do!" she yelled.

"You said you loved Lisa, but you're willing to kill her."

"Shut up!" he shouted. "Just shut up and — " Garrett stopped suddenly as a piercing cry tore through the air.

Melanie's scalp prickled at the sound.

Lisa was screaming.

Garrett turned, but he was too late. His breath came out in a hoarse rush as the chair rammed into him at top speed. The impact knocked him onto the grass and sent the knife flying from his hand.

Lisa was screaming.

Garrett moved fast, but Melanie was faster. Before he was on his feet, she stopped the chair, and pushed it farther down the sidewalk, away from him.

Then she grabbed the knife.

Now she was in charge.

Garrett's dark glasses had fallen off and his eyes were narrowed, watching the knife. He didn't move. He didn't speak.

Lisa suddenly stopped screaming — frozen in shock.

Melanie tightened her grip on the knife.

Suddenly, the silence was broken.

Car doors slammed. Footsteps pounded through soggy grass. A voice shouted, "Lisa? Lisa!"

Lisa's father tore around the corner of the house. Georgia Hudson and two policemen were behind him.

"Lisa!" Stuart Randolph shouted, racing up the walk. "I called from the airport — didn't get an answer! I got the police down the road to come up here with me." He stopped next to the wheelchair, looking back and forth between Lisa and Melanie. "I heard Lisa — heard her screaming. What happened?"

"It was Garrett," Melanie said, her voice shaking. She dropped the knife, but kept her eyes on Garrett. "He tried to kill us. He was going to shove us over the cliff!"

Georgia Hudson gasped. One of the police officers went quickly over to Garrett. Another picked up the knife.

"He killed a backpacker and buried his body in the woods," Melanie went on. She shivered violently. "Lisa saw it happen. She told me. And Garrett was going to kill us to keep us quiet."

"What do you mean, Lisa *told* you?" Georgia Hudson asked.

"She used the book I was reading. She tapped her hand on certain words and sentences." Melanie shivered again and wrapped her arms around herself. "I knew it had to be something horrible that happened but I didn't figure out *how* horrible until today. When I found the body."

"The body?" the police officer near her repeated. "You found a body?"

Melanie waved behind her, toward the woods. "It's — he's — back that way. It's easier if you go around on Route Nine and follow the trail in from the old road. There's a clearing and then — " she swallowed " — and then, not much farther on, you'll find him. He's been dead awhile." She swallowed again. "His name was Peter."

The officer pulled a cellular phone from his jacket and called for backup. When he finished, he looked at Melanie. "I'm going to need the whole story."

Melanie hugged herself tighter. She couldn't stop shaking.

"She's almost in shock — let her tell you inside," Mr. Randolph demanded. "I want to get my daughter in the house, too."

As he lifted Lisa out of the wheelchair, Melanie reached out and took hold of her hand.

"We did it, Lisa," she murmured. "Everything will be all right now."

Lisa's eyes crinkled at the corners. She squeezed Melanie's hand. Then her father hurried with her up the steps and into the library.

Melanie followed. Halfway up the steps, she stopped and turned back.

Garrett hadn't moved. He stood on the grass staring at Melanie, as if he were the one who was paralyzed.

His eyes were like pale blue marbles, and just as empty.

Melanie shivered and went inside.

At the diner the next day, Trina peppered Melanie with questions. "Lisa screamed?" she asked. "She really screamed?"

Melanie nodded, swallowing a bite of cheeseburger. "Her father said it was a breakthrough. He called the doctor and told her, and the doctor was really excited. She said Lisa may be talking soon."

Trina went off to wait on another customer and Melanie ate some more of her cheeseburger. Maybe she'd have two — she hadn't been able to eat last night.

It had taken her a long time to get to sleep. Images of what had happened kept tumbling around in her mind, keeping her awake. Stumbling onto the body. Running through the woods. Garrett's dark glasses. The knife. Lisa's scream.

Melanie blinked the images away. It was

finally over. Trina came back and leaned her elbows on the counter. "What about the reading? I guess you won't be doing that anymore, huh?"

"Yes, I will," Melanie said. "Mr. Randolph called this morning and asked me if I'd be there on Monday. I said I would if my car was fixed by then. Actually, he said I could come whenever I want and I will. Not for money," she added. "I like Lisa. I think we'll be friends."

"Speaking of friends," Trina said. She nodded her head toward the door of the diner.

Melanie spun around.

Jeff Singer was standing in the doorway.

"Mel!" Trina whispered. "Don't you feel weird? I mean, you actually thought *he* was the one!"

Melanie stared at Jeff. She'd called him last night and told him everything. Even how she'd suspected him. He hadn't said much and she couldn't tell how he felt.

She could tell now, though. Jeff was smiling at her. She smiled back.

His dark eyes were warm and inviting.

Melanie spun back around and grinned at Trina. "I think he just *might* be the one," she said.

# About the Author

Carol Ellis is the author of more than twenty books for young people, including *Silent Witness*, *The Stepdaughter*, *The Window*, *My Secret Admirer*, *Camp Fear*, and the short story, "The Doll," in *Thirteen*. Some of her favorite reading is mystery and suspense, especially those books in which an ordinary, innocent person becomes caught up in something strange and frightening.

Carol Ellis lives in New York State with her husband and their son.

# THRILLERS

## D.E. Athkins
- ☐ MC45246-0 Mirror, Mirror — $3.25
- ☐ MC45349-1 The Ripper — $3.25
- ☐ MC44941-9 Sister Dearest — $2.95

## A. Bates
- ☐ MC45829-9 The Dead Game — $3.25
- ☐ MC43291-5 Final Exam — $3.25
- ☐ MC44582-0 Mother's Helper — $3.50
- ☐ MC44238-4 Party Line — $3.25

## Caroline B. Cooney
- ☐ MC44316-X The Cheerleader — $3.25
- ☐ MC41641-3 The Fire — $3.25
- ☐ MC43806-9 The Fog — $3.25
- ☐ MC45681-4 Freeze Tag — $3.25
- ☐ MC45402-1 The Perfume — $3.25
- ☐ MC44884-6 The Return of the Vampire — $2.95
- ☐ MC41640-5 The Snow — $3.25
- ☐ MC45680-6 The Stranger — $3.50
- ☐ MC45682-2 The Vampire's Promise — $3.50

## Richie Tankersley Cusick
- ☐ MC43115-3 April Fools — $3.25
- ☐ MC43203-6 The Lifeguard — $3.25
- ☐ MC43114-5 Teacher's Pet — $3.25
- ☐ MC44235-X Trick or Treat — $3.25

## Carol Ellis
- ☐ MC46411-6 Camp Fear — $3.25
- ☐ MC44768-8 My Secret Admirer — $3.25
- ☐ MC47101-5 Silent Witness — $3.25
- ☐ MC46044-7 The Stepdaughter — $3.25
- ☐ MC44916-8 The Window — $2.95

## Lael Littke
- ☐ MC44237-6 Prom Dress — $3.25

## Jane McFann
- ☐ MC46690-9 Be Mine — $3.25

## Christopher Pike
- ☐ MC43014-9 Slumber Party — $3.50
- ☐ MC44256-2 Weekend — $3.50

## Edited by T. Pines
- ☐ MC45256-8 Thirteen — $3.50

## Sinclair Smith
- ☐ MC45063-8 The Waitress — $2.95

## Barbara Steiner
- ☐ MC46425-6 The Phantom — $3.50

## Robert Westall
- ☐ MC41693-6 Ghost Abbey — $3.25
- ☐ MC43761-5 The Promise — $3.25
- ☐ MC45176-6 Yaxley's Cat — $3.25

---

Available wherever you buy books, or use this order form.

---

# THRILLERS